DREAMER'S WEB

MOONSHADOW BAY
BOOK 11

YASMINE GALENORN

A Nightqueen Enterprises LLC Publication

Published by Yasmine Galenorn

PO Box 2037, Kirkland WA 98083-2037

DREAMER'S WEB

A Moonshadow Bay Novella

Copyright © 2024 by Yasmine Galenorn

First Electronic Printing: 2024 Nightqueen Enterprises LLC

First Print Edition: 2024 Nightqueen Enterprises

Cover Art & Design: Ravven

Art Copyright: Yasmine Galenorn

Editor: Elizabeth Flynn

A Nightqueen Enterprises LLC Publication

Published in the United States of America

ACKNOWLEDGMENTS

Thanks to my usual crew: Samwise, my husband, Andria, and Jennifer. Without their help, I'd be swamped. To the women who have helped me find my way in indie, you're all great, and thank you to everyone. To my wonderful cover artist, Ravven, for the beautiful work she's done, and to my editor, Elizabeth, who helps me keep my ellipses under control—thank you both.

Also, my love to my furbles, who keep me happy. My most reverent devotion to Mielikki, Tapio, Ukko, Rauni, and Brighid, my spiritual guardians and guides. My love and reverence to Herne, and Cernunnos, and to the Fae, who still rule the wild places of this world. And a nod to the Wild Hunt, which runs deep in my magick, as well as in my fiction.

You can find me through my website at **Galenorn.com** and be sure to sign up for my **newsletter** to keep updated on all my latest releases! You can find my advice on writing, discussions about the books, and general ramblings on my **YouTube channel**. If you liked this book, I'd be grateful if you'd leave a review—it helps more than you can think.

January 2024
Brightest Blessings,
~The Painted Panther~
~Yasmine Galenorn~

WELCOME TO DREAMER'S WEB

It's a new year, and Killian and I are finally married. Ari's salon, in my old house, is nearly finished. My energy reflux syndrome (ERS) is still plaguing me, but my doctor has found the right mixture of herbs to neutralize as many of the symptoms as possible.

At work, we're following up on some UFO reports from around the area, though I have no intention on becoming a guinea pig in an alien's medical laboratory. But then, during my birthday party, something happens. Somebody gives me a present, one that comes with an unexpected—and unwelcome—surprise. I receive an antique mirror, a portal that sucks me into a realm from which shadow people and demons can emerge. Now, I must figure out who gave me the mirror, and I must face the shadow man from my childhood before he's able to latch onto me and drain me for good.

CHAPTER ONE

"HE'S PLANNING A SURPRISE PARTY, ISN'T HE?" I STARED down Ari. If I couldn't break my best friend, who could? I knew Killian was up to something for my birthday, but I hadn't been able to find out. "Tell me and he'll never know you're the one who snitched."

"No go," she said. "But good try!"

Ari curled up on the sofa, a patchwork throw spread over her legs. We were watching *Bluey*. Or rather, Ari's soon-to-be adopted daughter and son were watching *Bluey*. Emily was four, and LaKirk was two, and they were darlings...*for kids*. I was always vaguely uncomfortable with children, though I found some of them adorable, especially this pair.

LaKirk stumbled to his feet and, fixated on Xi and Klaus, who were curled up in a recliner, began tottering toward them at breakneck speed. It had never crossed my mind how fast toddlers could move, but this kid could win the Indy 500. With some innate sense of impending doom, Klaus and Xi woke and bounced off the sofa to race away. LaKirk screwed up his face and let out a wail.

"Oh, dear," Ari said, jumping up to scoop him up. She tried to soothe him, as well as scolding him to leave the kitties alone, but it wasn't working.

"The nanny will be here in ten minutes," she said to me, an apology in her voice.

"Not a problem." Actually, it *was* a problem, but I didn't want Ari to feel unwelcome. The shrieks of toddlers triggered my migraines, like most high-pitched noises that went on for too long. Emily looked like she was debating on whether to join LaKirk in his distress, or to return to the show. I decided to help her decision along and walked over to kneel beside her.

"So, you like Bluey?" I asked. I never talked baby talk to kids, because it felt awkward and weird. I did use it on the cats, but that was entirely different.

She glanced up at me, her blond curls bobbing. Both kids had that golden brown skin the often came from an interracial couple, but Emily had inherited her father's blond hair and blue eyes, and LaKirk had his mother's dark kinky hair and dark eyes. Their parents had emigrated from France a few years before the kids were born, and they had no relatives in the US, and in fact—none who were interested in them over in France, either.

Emily apparently decided that talking was better than screaming, so she nodded. "LaKirk likes Bluey better than I do, though."

"What's your favorite show?" I asked, as Ari carried LaKirk into the kitchen.

Scrunching up her face, Emily thought for a moment. "*Beat Bobby Flay*," she said. "He cooks circles around his 'ponents."

Beat Bobby Flay? The kid liked a cooking show over cartoons?

"Well, that's a surprise," I said. "I'd never have guessed

that." I wasn't sure where to go next, so I finally asked, "Do you want to be a cook when you grow up?"

"I want to have a cooking show on TV," she said. "I want to host *Top Chef*."

"Well, you have big goals." When I was her age, I barely knew what I wanted for breakfast.

"Mo... Meagan is teaching me how to cook," she said, proudly puffing out her chest. But I had caught the slip. She had almost called Meagan "Mommy."

The kids had lost their parents during a home invasion. The robbers had gotten away with a thousand bucks. Ari and Meagan were their designated guardians and they were in the process of adopting the children formally. I didn't mention the slip. The less we focused on it, the more natural it would be for the children to transition over to new parents, in a new home.

"Oh yeah? What are you learning to cook?"

Emily brightened. "I can make toast and we make cookies together," she said.

At that moment, the doorbell rang and I left Emily to watch the show while I answered the door. It was Donna, the nanny. Ari brought the kids to work with her several days a week, and she and Meagan used some of the funds the parents had left to care for the kids to hire a nanny. It was easier than Meagan trying to take them into her job as the dean of women's sports at Bellingham Technical Community College.

"Come in." I opened the door, letting Donna in. She was in her twenties, a bear shifter like Meagan, and she had graduated from a one-year intensive course at the college preparing nannies to take care of children. That was how she had come to work for Ari and Meagan—she had been in one of the phys-ed classes that Meagan oversaw.

"Morning, January. Are they—there's my girl!" She knelt

3

so Emily could run up to her and throw her arms around Donna's neck. "How are you this morning?"

"Good. I had waffles for breakfast."

"Well, that sounds good. Where's Ari? Where's LaKirk?"

"LaKirk was throwing a fit so they're in the kitchen," I volunteered.

Emily brushed her hair back. "Can you ponytail me?"

"I will in a moment. I'm going to go talk to Ari." Donna headed for the kitchen.

Emily looked at me, an uncertain look on her face.

"Do you want me to put your hair in a ponytail? I wear my hair that way a lot," I added.

She handed me over the hair tie and turned around. I smoothed her hair back and carefully wrapped it into a ponytail, cautious not to pull the strands.

"There. How's that?"

"Thank you!" She hugged me, then went to pick up her hot pink backpack. Within moments, Ari and Donna returned, Donna holding a weepy LaKirk. Ari gathered up the diaper bag. LaKirk had been almost potty-trained, but since the death of their parents, he had regressed. So, Ari and Meagan still carried diapers with them. Ari gave me a hug.

"It was good to see you. Drop over for lunch, if you like. I don't have any clients between noon and one." She reached for Emily's hand.

"I'd like to, but I'm headed in to work today. I've been able to resume about 80 percent of my normal schedule, thanks to the meds that Dr. Fairsight has me on. Unless I've got a migraine, I've been going in five days a week, from ten until five. Have a great day. I'll peek in if you're still there when I get home."

Ari and Donna led the kids out the door, heading across the driveway to my old house. She had turned it into a salon and, with the help of the insurance money from Emily and LaKirk's parents—which came through faster than we expected—she had kicked the construction into high gear. Last week, she had been able to open the doors and escort her first client—me—in for a color and cut. The upstairs was still the same, and Donna entertained the kids up there during the day until Ari was done and could take them home, come evening.

As I shut the door, I had to acknowledge that I missed being able to hang out without the kids, but at least Ari was still in my life. And the kids really *were* cute, for kids. I turned around to find Xi and Klaus back in their favorite chair. They shot me accusatory looks and I grimaced.

"I'm sorry. You have to give them some slack—" I stopped as my phone rang. It was Rowan, my grandmother.

"Hello?" I walked over to the window, staring out into the front yard. It was mid-January, and a few snowflakes had started to fall. We were heading into a deep freeze over the next week. A blast of arctic air was sweeping down from Canada through the Pacific Northwest and we were on the front line.

"First, I wanted to confirm that we're voting on the full moon on the new members for the Crystal Cauldron, so we need everybody there."

My grandmother was the High Priestess of the Crystal Cauldron, our coven that was the local branch of the Order of the Moon. The Order of the Moon was a paramilitary branch of Crown Magika, the ruling society over the witch-blood in society. While we were bound to laws of the land, we were also bound to the laws of Queen Heliesa, the Queen of Witches, and the heart of witchblood itself.

"I've got it on my calendar. The twenty-fifth." I paused. "So, what are you up to tomorrow night?" I was being as transparent as a window, but I couldn't help it. I was never sure about surprises, and Killian knew it. But I also knew he liked to make me happy, and I hadn't thought of anything for my birthday that I wanted to do.

Rowan laughed. "You're fishing, my dear, and the pond is empty. I'll talk to you later." She hung up before I could ask a different way.

I pocketed my phone with a chuckle. Rowan could read me like a book, and she wasn't going to budge. "Fine," I said to the silent phone, and headed into the bedroom to finish getting ready for work. I was wearing a pair of black gauchos. They might not be in style, but they suited my body and personal look. I paired them with a cobalt blue sweater and knee-high black leather boots.

After touching up my makeup, I swallowed my morning meds—an herbal concoction compounded for members of the witchblood against severe migraines—and shrugged into a leather jacket with a fleece liner. Slinging my purse over my shoulder, with keys in hand, I made sure the stove was off and locked the door behind me as I headed to work.

CONJURE INK WAS ON THE MOVE AGAIN. WE'D MOVED OUT of a mini-mall that had ended up with a major plumbing/flooding problem, into a house that my boss bought. Now, we were looking for a new space again. The house was fine, but since Caitlin and Tad had finally proclaimed their love, she was moving in. Obviously, they wanted a private home in which to begin their relationship and that meant either they looked for a new place together, or the business moved back into its own space. Given we already had jury-rigged offices and storage, it seemed easier to return to an actual office. It would also free Tad from living at work.

But, for the moment, we were still here. I parked, grabbed my drink—a triple-shot latte with sugar-free caramel, whipped cream, and a sprinkle of cinnamon—and hustled to the door.

Wren was at her desk. "Hey, good to see you." She was smiling, which meant that Walter was having a good day. Her husband had been diagnosed with multiple sclerosis not all that long ago, and the disease had progressed rapidly. He had good days and he had bad days. And the bad days were bad. Luckily, Wren had help with him, a home health care aide to watch Walter during the days when she was at work. It gave her a little break as well.

"You too. How's Walter?"

"He's hanging in there," she said, accepting the doughnut I handed her from the pastries I'd bought at the coffee shop. After chatting some more, I headed into the living room that we used as a main office.

Tad, Caitlin, and Hank were at the round table where we held our meetings. As I dropped off my purse and jacket at my desk, Wren followed me, sitting at the table. I settled in and pulled out my tablet, taking another sip of the latte.

"It's nice to have you back, January," Tad said. "While we can manage without you, it doesn't feel the same."

I flashed him a smile. "Thanks. I've missed being here." I had gone down to three days a week, and sometimes not even that. But the new drugs were working wonders, and the herbs and regular magical practice had driven the migraines back to a handful of days a month. "What have we got this week?"

"There were a string of UFO sightings near Bloedel Donovan Park on Lake Whatcom. It's a twenty-minute drive from Moonshadow Bay, so we're making arrangements for later this week to interview people who were there," Hank said. He texted us the information. "I thought I might drive over and spend an evening staking out the area. It appears that the sightings have all taken place between one to three A.M., over the lake. There's no guarantee I'd see anything, but I'm willing to try."

"Isn't it a little cold for a stakeout?" Caitlin asked.

"Yeah, but I have a warm truck and I can always sleep in the back in a sleeping bag." Hank shrugged. He was a hearty man, with years of camping out and roughing it behind him. "I figure I might as well get out there tonight, while we're still getting reports."

"Take your phone and make certain you keep alert. We don't want somebody beating the crap out of you for your vehicle." Tad pulled up his calendar. "What about Saturday? It seems to be the day that's best for most of our interview subjects."

"Works for me," I said. "Depending on whether I'm able." I sighed. *Everything* depended on whether I was feeling okay. I felt so unreliable, it wasn't funny.

ERS—energy reflux syndrome—affected those who were born with witchblood who hadn't been allowed, or able, to use their magic regularly enough. I hadn't even seen an Aseer until a couple years ago, when my mother should have had me tested as a child.

She hadn't been ashamed of my blood, but afraid that the curse on our family would catch me sooner somehow if I used my magic more. We'd never know if she had been right, but now I had to cope with a chronic illness. At least the doctor had helped me manage it now.

"We'll play it by ear," Tad said. "Oh, are you going to be in tomorrow?"

Surprised, I frowned. I hadn't expected that question. "As far as I know. Why?"

"Because it's your birthday and I thought you might have plans." Tad rapped his knuckles on the table.

"Not that I know of," I said. "Am I supposed to?" I wondered if Killian had gotten to him. But I didn't want to be a broken record and interrogate every person I knew. Come to think about it, on the off-chance I was wrong, I didn't want to sound like an idiot, either.

Caitlin laughed. "Are we done with the meeting? I need to update the website."

"Have we found a new office yet?" I asked.

"We're close. In fact, we're going to see it this afternoon. I want you guys to be comfortable there, and I want your input, January. The office building is old—historical, you might say, for Moonshadow Bay. It's near our old office, but in a separate building. It's not a bad price, either."

"How much is the rent?" Hank asked.

"No rent. If I like it, I'm buying it," Tad said. He was rich —or rather, his family was. But he loved his work and his family appreciated that he had found his passion, so they had signed over a part of his trust fund early and he used that to help the business thrive. We brought in enough to cover mortgage and salaries, usually, but Tad made sure that we were able to go deep into the research that was our primary focus, rather than the clientele side.

"If we move on the weekend, Killian will help—unless he's on call at the clinic." I picked up my tablet and coffee. "We're done, then?"

Tad nodded. "If you'd start writing up the articles for the website, I'd appreciate it."

"Not a problem." Tad had assigned me the task of writing some articles about the urban legends we'd investigated and discovered to be true. Since my background was in writing and publishing, it was the most fun I'd had in ages. I loved my job, but it was nice to have a break from fighting ghosts and running from beasties.

As I settled myself in front of the keyboard, I whispered a prayer of thanks. Even with the migraines, I had a wonderful life. And though I knew that everything could change on a dime, I wanted the universe to know I was grateful.

CHAPTER TWO

By the time we were ready to go visit the new office building, I'd managed to finish ten short reports for the website. That was a drop in the bucket, considering we were revamping the entire site, but it was a start.

"Let's ride together," Tad said. "Unless anybody has to leave early?"

Nobody did, so we piled into the company van and, with Tad driving, headed out. I leaned back in my seat. Caitlin and I sat next to the equipment bay. Wren sat on the floor, next to me, her legs crossed. Hank rode shotgun.

"So, have you made plans for your honeymoon yet? Or are you waiting for a while?" Wren asked.

Killian and I had put off our honeymoon, opting to take a brief trip out of town instead.

"We're thinking of taking a trip over to the peninsula during the autumn, but we haven't decided anything yet." I shrugged. "After the clusterfuck of a wedding, we just wanted to decompress. I mean, it was beautiful, but thanks to Ellison, it wasn't exactly what we'd anticipated."

"Yeah, he should write into Reddit. *Am I the asshole for trying to murder my ex at her wedding?*" Caitlin snorted.

"Thank gods, he's in prison and won't see the light of day for a long time."

Ellison had received a thirty-five-year minimum sentence for trying to kill me, and the fact that he'd also been convicted of attacking Killian, and that he'd been an asshole to the judge in court had added fifteen years to his sentence, for a grand total of fifty years, without possibility of parole before then.

In my dark heart, I rejoiced. If he ever managed to get released, he'd be over ninety and it would be a lot harder for him to hurt anybody.

"Well, I have news," Wren said. "The doctor's started Walter on an experimental medication, since his case is progressing so rapidly, and he's already showing some response. It's controversial, but given the speed of the MS's progression, we figured he should give it a try." She smiled, though the tension was apparent.

I thought about asking more about the medication, but I didn't want to cause her any anxiety. Life-threatening conditions were terrifying to face, and she and Walter were doing their best to adapt to their new paradigm. So I squeezed her shoulder, settled back in my seat, and played with my phone.

Ten minutes later, we pulled into a parking lot in front of a small office building. It wasn't attached to any other structure, which meant we wouldn't be at the mercy of neighbors, and it was one story with a lot of windows. The building was red brick, and while it had obviously been updated, I could see the hints that it was far older than it looked. As Tad parked and we exited the van, I glanced around at the parking lot. A D-Cup Java stand sat on the other side of the lot, which held sixteen cars, eight on either side.

"D-Cup Java? *Really?*" Caitlin asked.

Tad blushed. "I didn't realize what it was at first. But we're not buying the coffee shop." He brandished his cane, flourishing it before heading toward the building. His recovery from the damage sustained on our ill-chosen adventure over six months ago had been slow—a lot slower than expected. He'd been angry at first, suppressing it, but now he accepted where he was. *Day by day*, he said. It seemed we were all fighting our private demons.

I snickered. D-Cup Java was a holdover from a decade ago when somebody decided to basically create the Hooters for the coffee world. Scantily clad young women with big breasts, small waists, and the ability to tolerate a chill hung out of the drive-thru windows, offering coffee, their boobs barely constrained by cropped shirts tied with a tenuous knot in the center. They tendered up wide smiles with your coffee, and I had seen a few men tip them by tucking a dollar or so between their boobs.

"Well, at least it's caffeine," I said. I wanted coffee but how far was I willing to go for it? I turned to Hank. "You want to grab coffee for us?"

He gave me one of those *seriously?* looks. "You want me to go over there and stare at half-nekkid women hoping to cadge an extra dollar out of me for flashing their boobs?"

"They aren't flashing them, but it feels odd for me to do it. I mean, I have boobs that size, why would I want to look at somebody else's?" I sighed. "Fine, I'll do it."

"Let me," Caitlin said. "What do you want?"

We gave her our orders as Tad unlocked the main door. "There's a back door, as well," he said. "Come in. Caitlin, hurry back!"

"I will," she said, waving as she darted over the concrete bumper blocks in the parking lot, landing on the sidewalk beyond. She strode up to the coffee shop—well, stand, it wasn't an actual shop—and waved her credit card at the bombshell blonde who took her order.

I started to follow Tad and Hank into the building. Wren hung back. She gnawed on her lip.

I turned away from the door. "Is something wrong, Wren?"

"I don't know. I have an uneasy feeling. To be honest, Walter wanted to take the medicine, but I don't feel comfortable about it. Not only is it experimental, but I...my intuition is screaming *No—don't*! But how do I crush his hopes? I can't offer an alternative. So I'm keeping my mouth shut."

"What do you think might happen?" I knew, though. I knew that Wren was afraid that the meds might worsen Walter's condition, or maybe even kill him.

"I have a feeling there's some really bad side effect they haven't discovered yet. It's been out a year, and they're still doing clinical trials on it. Walter fits the criteria—it's for rapidly progressing autoimmune diseases. He wants to help advance research." She gave me a plaintive look. "What do I do?"

I didn't know what to say. It wasn't something I could decide. But I finally asked, "Do you think he'll regret not trying it?"

"I'm sure he will," she said softly. "In some people, MS progresses slowly. But Walter's declining a lot faster than they originally thought he would. If I tell him no, he'll lose hope. He's trying to hang onto the good, but in his position, I can see how rough it is. I live with it, I'm impacted by his condition, but I can't ever know just what he's going through."

I paused, then said, "Do you mind me being blunt here?"

"Please do."

"My condition isn't nearly as debilitating as Walter, but the ERS—it's not easy. I'm here today because of the new herbal concoction that Dr. Fairsight came up with. If she hadn't stumbled onto the mixture, I'd still be kicking it at home with at least half the month spent in a migraine haze."

Wren stared at the ground. "Yeah, I hear you."

"Chronic illness strips parts of you away, and sometimes it doesn't stop till it feels like you're a shell of who you used to be. If this gives Walter hope, and if he'll continue to decline without the potential for help, I think you need to let him explore it." I added, "This is something I never understood. Not really—not fully. Not until I developed a condition myself. It's easy to be angry at others for not understanding, but there's a point where you have to walk through the fire to fully comprehend what living with a chronic illness means. You can empathize, worry, cry, and agonize with someone you love who has a chronic condition, but you can never walk in their shoes unless you develop something equitable."

Wren inhaled sharply, then let out a long breath. "You're right. Okay, thanks, January. I think I can handle it better when you explain it like that. I'll keep my peace and pray to all the gods that the meds don't do anything bad to him." She glanced over at Caitlin, who was trying to balance a tray of drinks. "I'm going to help her. Why don't you go in? I need a minute to clear my thoughts."

As I entered the main reception room, I could feel the history behind the building. It had been renovated, which could stir up spirits, but it had the feel of its history behind it. The space was a blank slate, though. There was no reception desk, nothing except floors, walls, and doors.

"Well?" Tad asked expectantly.

"Well, what?"

"What do you feel? Why don't you wander around for a

while?" He sounded more excited than a kid on Christmas morning.

I waited till Wren and Caitlin joined us, accepted my latte, then began poking around.

The building was one story, with no basement or attic. There was a ceiling crawlspace, but it wasn't an attic. As I wandered through the rooms, I strained to hear anything floating on the astral. I caught the faint sounds of a piano, and of tapping shoes, but that was it. The brick had absorbed the energy from the past, but instead of being uneasy, it made me smile. I caught a hint of laughter and the words "Let's start again, children..."

"What was this building before it was sold?" I asked.

"It's been empty for about five years. Before that, it belonged to a real estate company for twenty years. That takes us back to 1999. Before that... Let me see." Tad consulted notes on his tablet. "From 1970 through 1999 it was a restaurant—Tiny Bob's Burger Barn. From 1964 through 1970 it was empty. From 1950 through 1964, an accounting firm owned it. And from 1932 through 1949, the building was Miss Penny's Dance & Music Academy for Children."

That made sense. "Nothing traumatic happened here, right? That we know of?"

"Not that I could find, and I looked. Why, what are you sensing?"

I took a deep breath and lowered myself into trance. Once again, I began to sense the laughter and music, and what I now recognized as the sound of shoes tapping. I caught a glimpse of an older, white-haired woman playing the piano, as a line of mini-ballerinas pirouetted and leapt their way across the room, pink tutus fluttering in the astral wind. There was nothing more there—nothing sinister, nothing hiding in the shadows.

Exhaling softly, I opened my eyes and smiled. "We have

memories locked in here, but they're good ones. Happy ones, nice for a change. Whoever Miss Penny was, her students loved their time here, and she enjoyed teaching them. The laughter and joy from those years are locked within the walls, and there's no need to exorcise them. They can only make our work happier."

Tad looked relieved, as did the others. "Thank gods. For once, we're not fighting to reclaim space from the spirit world. So you like it?"

I looked around again. Wren would once again have an enclosed reception area. We, as we liked it, would have a big office for all of us. There were three more rooms besides the bathroom. One could be for camera and equipment storage, one could be a break room, and one could be a supply room. The break room had space for a kitchenette to be installed. The main office was big enough so that if we expanded staff in the future, we wouldn't be crowded.

"I like it. It feels comfy to me."

"Me too," Hank said, looking around. "It has potential for the future."

Tad turned to Caitlin and Wren. "What about you two?"

They both enthusiastically agreed.

"Then we're good to go," he said. "I'll contact the real estate agent and buy the building. Meanwhile, Caitlin, decide what we need for the equipment room to safely store all our gear. Wren, check out the storeroom and make a list of shelving and storage we'll need. January, if you would make a list of what we'll need for the break room, and Hank—you'll be in charge of planning what kind of security system we'll need—how many cameras, what kind of surveillance...you know the drill."

He opened his messenger bag and handed us each a tape measure and a notepad. "Measure twice so we cut once. I am quite willing to employ a firm to install everything, but we need to know what we want, first." Pulling out his phone, he took off to the other side of the room to negotiate in private.

I headed into the break room.

It was bare—not even so much as a cabinet. It occurred to me that we usually ate in the main room, but it was nice to have a separate area for meetings and for meals. I began jotting down notes. We'd bring our round table, but we used that for meetings, so we'd need a break room table and chairs. We'd also need a fridge, a stove, a cabinet and counter, sink, cupboards, microwave, toaster oven, coffee station. As the list grew, I began to have glimpses of what the room could look like. I listed ideas for colors and artwork. The longer I walked around the empty space, the more the completed room grew in my mind.

By the time I returned to the others, Tad was off the phone. He gave me a thumbs-up.

"We've got it! I asked for a quick closing, so when we get back to the office, if you could start calling renovators. You've been through that with your old house, so you know who does good work." He was grinning ear to ear. I had the feeling part of his joy was coming from realization that Caitlin would be moving in with him soon.

Fifteen minutes later, we were all ready to go. Tad dropped us off at the current office, and then—taking his own car—headed toward the Realtor's office to fast-track the paperwork. He had the money to speed up things and wasn't afraid to use it.

It was nearing three. I realized that we'd skipped lunch and headed into the kitchen. "Anybody hungry besides me?"

"I could eat a bite," Hank said, following me in. Caitlin and Wren were hungry, too, so I retrieved a loaf of bread, deli turkey and ham, mayo, mustard, and ketchup, a container of sliced tomatoes, and some cheese out of the fridge. Hank helped me carry everything to the table, then he returned to the kitchen for plates and knives, and we gathered around to make sandwiches.

"So, what do you make of the UFO reports?" I asked Hank. "Do you think they're real?"

"They sound pretty consistent, from the initial reports," he said, biting into his sandwich.

Caitlin finished making a turkey sandwich and slid the bread over to me. "What are your opinions on UFOs, if you have any? I don't think we've ever talked about them, other than in general terms."

It was true. While we were heavily into investigating urban legends, my specialty was focused on spirits and ghosts. We hadn't tackled the UFO sightings. Well, except for Hank. He'd seen UFOs at least twice in his life—once when he was young, another when he was older, on a hiking trip with his parents.

"I don't know," I said, thinking about it. What *did* I believe about UFOs? "When I talked to Bonnie Craghorn, her theories made a lot of sense to me."

Bonnie Craghorn lived up in Terameth Lake, another shadow town like Moonshadow Bay or Whisper Hollow. Shadow towns were on the edge between worlds. They were usually havens for Otherkin and magical energy. My maternal great-grandparents had been some of Moonshadow Bay's founders.

"What's that? I don't remember hearing about it," Wren asked.

"She believes UFOs are creatures coming through portals from other dimensions. They're silent, they move swiftly, they vanish without warning." It really did make sense, though it didn't explain everything.

"What about the Grays and other creatures seen coming out of the portals?" Hank asked.

"I don't know, honestly. I haven't thought about this

much. Maybe they're creatures who transport other creatures in their bellies? Maybe the ships themselves are sentient? I doubt we'll ever fully know until we examine one." I frowned. "What about the new reports coming from the government? The ones that were declassified a few months ago? Have you read any of those yet?"

"There are so many it will take me months to go through them, if not years. I think over fifteen hundred were made available," Hank said. He paused, then said, "What about if I pick out a couple each day for you that I think you'll find interesting, and we can talk them over. We could start tomorrow."

I wasn't enthusiastic about the idea—primarily because I knew it would be full of bureaucratic language—but he seemed excited, so I decided what the hell.

"Sure thing," I said. "We'll start tomorrow."

With that, we cleaned up and got back to work. Tad texted to say he'd be tied up all afternoon and for us to lock up when we were done. And Caitlin would stay after to wait for him. The light in her eyes made me happy that they'd finally put their fears aside and discovered their feelings for one another.

CHAPTER THREE

BY THE TIME I ARRIVED HOME, KILLIAN WAS THERE.
Surprised, I cautiously navigated the ice forming on the sidewalk as I headed toward the door. The clouds were packing in. We were due for a freeze. We didn't have much snow on the ground, but that only made it worse. We had water from melting snow, and if that water froze, we'd have an ice slick the next morning.

As I opened the door, the smells of tomato sauce and parmesan swept over me and my mouth began to water.

"What smells so good?" I called out as I dropped my bag and coat on the sofa and leaned over to kiss Klaus, who was snoozing on the back of the leather couch. I headed into the kitchen.

Killian was stirring a sauce on the stove. Spaghetti noodles were bubbling in the stock pot, a salad filled the wooden salad bowl, and a gorgeous cake sat on the crystal cake plate. The ivory icing looked like Swiss buttercream, and blue roses decorated it. My name was written in icing on the top, and silver luster dust shimmered around the edges.

"I can't believe you did this!" I crossed behind the counter, and he held out one arm to draw me in for a kiss.

Killian was gorgeous. He had wavy wheat-colored hair that hung below his shoulders, and brilliant green eyes that matched my own. At six feet tall and sturdy, he was my mate and husband. He was also a wolf shifter. In fact, come Saturday night, Killian would be inducted as a second lieutenant in the Rainier Wolf Pack. He had been dubbed as one of the *noble alphas*.

Only a select handful of members—both male and female —ever attained that status, and it was from that group that the leaders were chosen. Killian had blossomed in the Pack— it was progressive, for wolf shifters—and now he was being rewarded for the work he'd put into it. It would be a semi-formal event and I was going to spend Saturday morning shopping for a dress.

"Oh, hell," I said, suddenly remembering we were slated to go gather UFO witness statements on Saturday morning.

"What's wrong, love? Did you want something else for dinner?" He looked crestfallen.

"No, this is perfect. I remembered something I need to take care of. Luckily, I can do it tomorrow," I said.

Tad wouldn't object to me skipping the day. I could always plead a headache, but he was a good guy and he'd understand. I didn't want to end up with a migraine by talking to highly emotional people. I was good at warding, and my grand-mother Rowan was helping me learn to be even better. But my empathy made me prone to lower my defenses without realizing it.

"Can I set the table?" I asked.

"No, you may not. Dinner will be ready in half an hour. Meanwhile, go into the master bath, please." He nodded toward the door. "I'll come get you when it's time to eat."

I kissed him again. "I'm hungry for more than dinner," I whispered.

"Dessert will have to wait, woman. Go, now." He winked at me, but the tone in his voice was firm and it made me want him even more. Killian was growing into his alpha status, but he never intruded on my autonomy, nor did he dismiss me as an equal partner.

Curious, I headed for the bedroom. Xi was asleep on the bed, her gorgeous tortie fur plush and soft. I nuzzled her, then opened the bathroom door. It was steamy inside, and smelled like vanilla. We had a walk-in shower that was luxurious, with a rain shower head, and a separate spa tub. The tub was filled with steaming water, with a few rose petals scattered on the surface, along with vanilla-scented bubbles.

Candles—battery operated—flickered around the room, and a goblet of iced sparkling cider sat on the side of the tub. A loose comfy blue chemise was draped over the garment rack, along with my fleece robe.

I wanted to run out and give Killian another hug but decided to take advantage of the steaming water. I undressed and slid into the tub, immersing myself in the warmth. After the chill of the outside, the water wrapped me like a warm embrace. Leave it up to Killian to prepare something like this for my birthday.

Leaning back, I closed my eyes, letting the strain of the day ease up. I used to be able to handle full days of work, but now, even though my headaches were better, the days took their toll. I leisurely slid the sponge down my arms, wondering if I'd ever fully be my old self—no worries, no cares, no concerns about overdoing. A twinge in my heart told me that those days were gone, and a melancholy shroud surrounded me, making me want to cry.

For all my advice to Wren, I did understand how Walter felt.

I gave in and let tears slide down my face. I was happy, truly happy with Killian, but it felt like my life had shattered and I was trying to find all the puzzle pieces. Some were missing, and some had ragged edges now, and I didn't know how to make them fit.

Thanks to the doctor, my migraine days were cut in half, but that was still a solid week to ten days that I could expect to be laid up. A solid week to ten days that I used to have for myself, that I didn't have to pay tribute to the ERS. Chronic illness sucked in so many ways that I had never even thought about before. I tried to stave off the depression. I tried to be grateful for the good things in my life, but sometimes the differences between who I used to be and who I was now flattened me emotionally.

"Love, dinner's ready——" Killian froze as he peeked in the room. I suddenly realized that my eye makeup had started to run. "What's wrong?" He was at the edge of the tub in seconds. "What can I do? Are you all right? Are you hurt?"

I tried to dash away my tears, but he caught hold of my wrists, gently holding them away from my face. "Tell me what's going on," he said.

I caught a deep breath, letting it out slowly. "It's nothing," I whispered, not wanting to ruin the evening.

"No, it's *something*. Remember our vows—honesty above all else. What's wrong?" Killian sat on the side of the tub, slowly letting go of my arms. "Did I do something to upset you?"

I slid them back under the bubbles. I finally sighed.

"Okay, I'll tell you—and no, it's nothing you've done or not done. I'm not dealing well with the fact that I have to face living with the ERS for the rest of my life. I thought I'd accepted it, but today, for some reason, it's at the forefront of my mind."

I wiped my hands on the towel next to the tub, then used

it to dash away my tears. A black smudge from my eyeliner came off onto the towel.

"I'm not going to say I fully understand, but however I can help, please ask. I'm here for whatever you need, even if it's only to listen."

"I'll be all right," I said. "I'm hypersensitive tonight, which may mean a migraine is looming in the near future. As long as it waits until my birthday's over, I'll be okay. I need to accept that there are some things I can't control and get on with life." I sniffed. The smell of tomato and cheese filtered into the bathroom. "You said dinner's ready? It smells wonderful. I'll be out in a couple minutes."

"If you're sure—I'll go finish setting the table." Killian leaned down and kissed the top of my head.

"Go, I'll see you in a moment. I'm hungry, so I hope you made plenty." I waved him off, grateful for his concern, yet it was time to get tough with myself. There were days that were going to suck more than others, but I was tired of listening to myself complain.

As Killian headed out of the bathroom, I got out of the tub and took a quick rinse under the shower, then dressed in my nightgown and robe. I fixed my makeup and joined Killian for dinner. An oblong-shaped wrapped box was by my plate. I sat down, glancing at Killian, smiling.

"Thank you—I didn't expect this."

"I thought it would be more of a surprise the night *before* your birthday. That way we can go out tomorrow night if you like." He beamed. "Open the gift."

I slid the card out of the envelope. It had a gorgeous long-stemmed red rose on it, and inside, the sentiment read, *To the woman who made my dreams come true. Happy Birthday, and I love you.* Killian had signed it, *Love, your lucky, lucky husband.*

Smiling, I set the card against the salad bowl where I could see it and opened the package. Inside, was a slender rectangular jewelry box. As I opened it, I gasped. The candle-light glimmered against the sparkling blue diamond pendant on a silver chain. The pendant was shaped like an orchid, with the blue diamond—about a carat in size—sparkling in the center.

"Oh, Killian, this matches my wedding ring!" My wedding ring set had knotwork filigree around the band, holding alternating clear and blue diamonds that buttressed the center blue diamond. The wedding band matched the engagement band.

"That's why it caught my eye. I asked them to make the chain long enough so that you can easily drape it over your head. It will make it easier to get on and off if you have a migraine." His expression told me that he was pleased with my reaction. He reached out and took my hand. "I was hoping you'd like it. Happy birthday, love."

"Happy birthday, indeed," I said. "You *were* planning a surprise. You really managed to throw me off-base this time. Congratulations." I couldn't help but smile as I spoke. I slid the pendant over my head and sighed. "This is perfect. Thank you—for the dinner and the bath and the pendant. And for being you. I love you so much."

He brought my hand to his lips and kissed my fingers. "And I love you."

As we ate, I let his love cushion my melancholy. After dinner, as Killian led me into the bedroom and made love to me, I felt oddly shy. Romance had a way of making me feel vulnerable, in a way that I both feared and loved. And regardless of the energy reflux syndrome, I considered myself the luckiest woman in the world.

NEXT MORNING, I COULD STILL FEEL A MIGRAINE ON THE outskirts, but it wasn't here yet. I could probably manage work and, with a glimmer of luck, I'd manage to ward it off for good. I dressed in a black turtleneck and skirt, knee-high black boots, and I wore my new pendant. As I brushed my hair back behind a sparkling blue headband and put on my makeup, I decided that forty-three was shaping up to be a good year.

Killian was buttering English muffins, and he pointed to a plate with sausage patties on it. "Did you want a sausage breakfast sandwich?"

"Two if we have enough."

He shook his head. "Sorry, we have to go grocery shopping. I found enough muffins for two sandwiches. I can use bread, if you want—"

"Nope, don't sweat it. I can get a second on the way to work," I said as an alert told me someone had texted me. I glanced at the screen. It was from Tad.

CAN YOU COME IN NOW? WE HAVE AN EMERGENCY— DON'T WORRY, BUT IT IS URGENT. GET HERE ASAP, IF YOU WOULD. I'LL PROVIDE BREAKFAST.

ON MY WAY, I texted back.

"Listen, I have to go. I'll grab breakfast at the office. See you tonight, love. Please feed the cats before you go!" I plastered a quick kiss on Killian's cheek and headed for the car, carefully navigating the ice and a thin layer of snow that had fallen. As I put the car into gear and eased out of the driveway, I wondered what the hell could have happened.

CHAPTER FOUR

ONCE I GOT TO THE OFFICE, I HURRIED TOWARD THE DOOR. Wren was at her desk and she motioned for me to head into the living room. As I did, I looked around, trying to figure out what the emergency was. But nobody was at their desks. I glanced back at the foyer where Wren was focused on her computer.

"What's going on? Did I miss something? Was I supposed to meet Tad somewhere else?" Something felt off, though I wasn't sure what.

Wren stood and came in, frowning. "I'm not sure. Maybe he made a mistake?"

I set my purse on the table. "Well, I'm hungry. Is there anything for breakfast? I hurried out the door so fast I left my—"

"Did somebody ask for breakfast?" Tad barged through the front door. He was followed by Caitlin, Hank, Ari and the kids, Rowan, Tarvish, Teran, and Killian. They were carrying bags and gift-wrapped boxes and Caitlin had a tray full of drinks, as did Hank.

"What? What's going on?" I asked. I turned to Killian. "What are you doing here—and Rowan? Ari?"

The next moment, Tad set a huge rectangular box on the table and opened it to reveal a caterer's dream breakfast. "Happy birthday!"

I laughed. "Who put this together?"

"It was my idea," Ari said. "And everybody chipped in to help. Meagan would be here, if she could. But she sends her love."

The door opened, and Alicia King, a neighbor near me who had won a two-million-dollar lottery and had opened up a women's shelter with the proceeds, entered the room, followed by the members of the Crystal Cauldron.

I moved over to hug Killian. "I thought last night was—"

"I told Ari I wanted to make a special supper for you, and she suggested that you'd never expect *two* parties." Killian kissed me. "Go greet your guests. You deserve this." He gave me a gentle push on the small of my back.

Still speechless, I joined the throng at our meeting table. It was covered with bagels, fresh toast, and English muffins. For meat, there were sausages, bacon, smoked salmon, and ham, along with fresh eggs that someone had scrambled up in the kitchen. Pastries, muffins, hashbrowns, orange juice, fruit salad, and condiments completed the feast.

Ari handed me a plate and winked. I leaned over to kiss her cheek. "Thank you. Killian told me this was your idea."

"It was, but everybody helped," she said. "Happy forty-third!"

"Forty-three...wow. Well...life *is* getting better." I hadn't even thought about the change of years yet. But while forty had been a nightmare, the years since had gotten better. I threaded through the crowd, hugging my grandmother and her demon lover, greeting Alicia, kissing Caitlin on the cheek.

"Presents! Open your presents!" Nerium said, clapping.

A member of the Crystal Cauldron, Nerium was about as goth as you could get. Her sister, Yolen, was as light as Nerium was dark. Other members of the coven were here, as well; Berta, who was my grandmother's age, my aunt Teran, and Ari. Daya had been killed not long ago, and May—who had been older than my grandmother—had retired and given up her position. We were down two women, and we would need to fill the positions soon.

"I will! Give me a moment!" I said as Aunt Teran hustled over to give me a hug.

"We need to talk. Can we chat after your party, or do you need to get right to work?"

"I can take some time afterward. I wanted to talk to you, too. I heard from the lawyer from Nonny's estate. We'll be going through an intermediary." My grandmother had died in a plane crash, and she left her estate to me, but I wasn't about to keep it. She should have left it to Teran, her daughter. I was determined that my aunt was going to have it.

"That's what I wanted to chat about—I got a sheaf of paperwork from them." She glanced around. "I hope you're happy, dear. You deserve all the happiness in the world." With a sigh, she stroked my hair. Her own was waist-length and right now, it was a rainbow of unicorn pastels—pink, purple, gold. "I'm so happy you moved back to Moonshadow Bay."

"Me too. Now, I've got to open my presents before they start chanting."

With a grin, I moved over beside Nerium. We still didn't know each other too well, but I was growing more interested in my coven-mates. Especially now that Ari was busy with her children, and we had lost Daya. I hadn't given a lot of thought to Daya before, but the Covenant of Chaos had killed her, and that was enough to make me realize that, if I worked magic with someone, I should make the effort to get to know them better.

Nerium began handing me presents as I sat beside her. Each one was a lovely thought. There was some jewelry, makeup gift cards, a rose quartz bracelet from Rowan, a new brush and comb set, and then, Nerium handed me a large box that must have been sixteen inches wide by twenty inches long. I looked for a card, but there was none.

"Who do I have to thank for this?" I asked, but nobody claimed responsibility. Curious now, I opened the box and withdrew something large, cushioned in bubble wrap. My fingers immediately began to tingle. *Magic's afoot*, I thought.

I stripped away the bubble wrap to find a mirror. The moment I looked at it, it struck me as familiar, but I couldn't remember where, if anyplace, I had actually seen it. The frame was made of wood, with snakes that shrouded the oval mirror in the center. Hand-carved roses adorned the base of the frame, stained a deep burgundy. The thorns on their stems were gilt.

For some reason, the mirror disconcerted me, but it was beautiful and I didn't want whoever gave it to me to feel awkward, if they were here. Why any of my friends would keep it secret escaped me. But right now, I didn't have time to think about it. I set the mirror on the table.

"Thank you, whoever gave me the mirror. It's beautiful." I accepted the next gift from Nerium, and continued to open presents until they were done.

After the party, I sought out Teran while the others cleaned up. There was still a third of a cake but it would be gone by the end of the day. Killian left for work, as did Nerium and her sister Yolen. Alicia paused to say goodbye.

"Dear, it was so good to see you again." Alicia was witchblood, and while I didn't know how old she was, she looked elderly, which meant she could be two hundred years old or more.

Alicia lived in a tidy but weathered house a few blocks away from me, but once she won the lottery, she had spruced up her place and had bought a large Victorian on the outskirts of town and turned it into A Step Up, a nonprofit shelter for women and children who were the victims of domestic violence, or who were down on their luck. She was partnering with businesses in Bellingham, Moonshadow Bay, and several other small towns around the area to help pair women with job opportunities and low-income housing.

"How's the shelter doing?" I asked. I made it a point to donate monthly to her shelter, the food bank, and a couple pet rescue organizations around the area.

"We're operating at 70 percent capacity. I wish we weren't, simply because it would mean fewer women in need, but I'm glad we can be there for them." She paused, then added, "I'm so happy for you. Killian's a wonderful man, and you've really turned your life around."

I smiled. "Yeah, I guess I have." My life had been in a collapsed ruin when I returned home to Moonshadow Bay, but now I was thriving.

"Well, I'll see you around," Alicia said, waving as she headed for the door.

I turned to Teran. "What do you think about asking Alicia to join the Crystal Cauldron?"

"I don't know if Rowan would go for that. Alicia has strong powers, but she's too gentle for what we sometimes need," she answered. "You can ask your grandmother, though. Meanwhile, can we talk about the lawyer and the estate?"

I nodded, looping my arm through hers. "What's the timeline?"

"Any time we're both free, we can schedule a meeting with

the lawyers here in town. They'll conference in Nonny's lawyers. But before we do that, the lawyers did tell you that Nonny owned her estate in Ireland, and a cabin up near Mount Baker?"

I tilted my head. "Yeah, I remember them mentioning something about that."

"Apparently, the cabin's on a couple acres of land outside of Glacier. I had no clue, either. And I want you and Killian to have it. I'll take the estate in Ireland and probably sell it, but I want you to have the cabin, so you have a vacation home." She took my hands. "It's so sweet of you to sign over the estate to me, but I want to share with you."

I started to protest but she squeezed my fingers. "No—you're not going to change my mind. The cabin is yours." Motioning to the table filled with presents and leftover cake, she added, "Who gave you that mirror?"

"I have no idea. It's beautiful," I said, glancing at it. "But it makes me nervous. I don't know why—I feel like I've seen it before. Or something like it." Once again, I tried to recall where I'd encountered it, but a sudden jolt of migraine pain hit me. "Crap, I feel a migraine coming on."

"Maybe take the rest of the day off, if you can." Teran hugged me and kissed my cheek. "I'll set up the lawyers' meeting, if you like."

"Let me know when and where, and I'll be there." I headed over to Tad, the headache beginning to worsen. "Yo, Tad. A migraine's coming on. I first noticed it last night but thought it had backed off."

"Go home, rest. Take the rest of your pastries," he said, motioning to the table.

I laughed. "No, I'll leave it for all of you. I have leftover cake at home. But I might make myself a plate for lunch, because I have a feeling by then, I'll be sinking into a fog."

"Ask Hank to help you out to your car with your presents.

Happy birthday, January. I can't express how happy I am that you came to work with us." He patted me on the shoulder and headed for his desk.

I put together a plate for lunch, wrapped it in foil, then asked Hank to help me carry everything out to the car. As he placed the presents into my back seat, he paused. "Do you need me to come with you and make certain you get home?"

"I should be okay, but thanks."

"Okay, but call if you need anything. Happy birthday." He finished loading everything in my car. "I hope you feel better."

"I had a great time this morning. Hopefully this will pass and I'll be in tomorrow." I waited till he shut the door and then, giving him a wave, I texted Killian before heading for home.

KILLIAN HAD OFFERED TO COME RIGHT HOME BUT I TOLD him no, I'd be fine. But by the time I pulled in the driveway, the nausea was starting to hit me. My stomach lurched as I brought the car to a halt. I waited until it settled, then looked in the back at the presents. There wasn't anything in there that couldn't stay out in the cold, and I was feeling pressed for time. There was an urgency that preceded my migraines—a feeling of limited time before they hit and I'd be incapacitated.

"Crap, I have to hurry." I grabbed my purse, made sure the car was locked, and headed inside. By the time I reached the kitchen, I was fumbling to make sure I had my phone. I squinted as I brought it up, texting Ari. She'd be next door with the kids.

ARI, ARE YOU BACK AT THE SALON? CAN YOU COME OVER FOR A FEW MINUTES? I'M HEADED INTO A MIGRAINE AND I

DON'T THINK I HAVE ENOUGH TIME TO BREW THE TEA THE
DOCTOR GAVE ME. MY MEDS ARE IN THE BEDROOM BUT I
DON'T TRUST MYSELF TO MAKE SURE I GRAB THE RIGHT
BOTTLE.

I fumbled a water bottle out of the fridge and stumbled to
the bedroom, trying to undress along the way. I managed to
reach the bed when Ari texted back.

I'M ON THE WAY OVER. I HAVE MY KEY IN CASE YOU
LOCKED THE DOOR.

I had a key to both Ari's house and the salon, and she had
a key to our house. It's what good friends did. As I dropped
onto the mattress, I groaned and tried to find my sleep mask.
I couldn't even manage to close the curtains.

"January? Where are you?" Ari's voice came from the
front door. A moment later, she peeked into the bedroom,
then hurried to my side. "Oh sweetie, what do you need?"

"Tea...the tea the doctor gave me. My meds are on the
bedside table. Can you help me into my nightgown?" The
words came out in spurts, along with a squeak as the migraine
hit full force. "My sleep mask?"

"Here, hold out your arms."

As I did, she slid the pendant over my head and set it on
my dresser, in my jewelry tray. Next, she took my hair out of
the ponytail and put a stretchy headband on me so it wouldn't
pull too tightly on my head. Then she eased my turtleneck off
and unhooked my bra.

"Only a good friend would set my boobs free," I
attempted to joke.

"Ssh, no problem, love. Here. Stand up so I can unzip
your skirt." She helped me stand and unzipped my skirt, then
eased it down over my hips. I sat down again, shivering, and
she found my flannel nightgown with a V-neck. It was sleeve-
less and a size too big so I wouldn't feel constrained. Then

she unzipped my boots and removed them, along with my socks.

Meanwhile, I tried to keep it together, but I was near tears. Undressing could be jarring when everything hurt so bad I wanted to throw up.

Ari pulled down the covers and got me settled in, propped up on my pillows. She pulled the curtains closed and helped me put on my sleep mask. "I'll be back with your medicines." She knew—like Killian, Rowan, and Teran did—what I was supposed to take when I was spiraling into a migraine. "You stay here."

As I leaned back, grateful that I didn't have to make any decisions, Ari moved away. Xi landed on the bed—I could tell by her smell. All cats had a certain smell, dusty and comforting, but each one was slightly different. I knew Xi and Klaus by their smells alone, especially when I was in a migraine when everything was so heightened. I stroked her fur as she curled up beside me. Xi had taken to sleeping beside me when I had migraines, and she kept watch over me. Klaus was nearby, too, but he hung back and I could feel his concern.

"Here," Ari said, returning to the room. I pushed the mask up so I could see her. She motioned for me to hold out my hand and she dropped two capsules into my palm. Handing me a glass of ice water—it helped keep my nausea at bay—she said, "Drink up. I'll go get your tea. Do you need saltines?"

I nodded. Saltines were one of the few foods that settled my stomach when I was spiraling deep into migraine-land. "Thank you. What about the kids?"

She shrugged. "Donna's watching them over at the salon. I told them if they behave, they'll get ice cream after work. I was between clients when you texted, but Frieda's there today and she'll handle things till I get back. Now, wait just a moment."

I set the water glass on the nightstand and closed my eyes. "Can you text Killian and tell him I'm in bed and okay? I told him I was on my way home. I didn't even have a chance to bring in my gifts."

Ari brought me my tea, then she texted Killian. "I'll be right back," she said. A few moments later, she popped back in. "And I texted Teran and she's coming to sit with you until Killian gets home. I also found your keys and brought in your presents. I'll wait until Teran gets here, then head back to work."

I started to tell her that she could go now, but a wave of nausea hit so deep that I curled onto my side in a fetal position, clutching my stomach. Ari vanished and returned with a cool cloth, which she held to the back of my neck. As the nausea subsided and I lay back, exhausted, she arranged the cloth over my forehead after pulling my sleep mask back into place. She took my hand and held it until Teran got there, and then, with my aunt taking over, Ari headed back to work.

CHAPTER FIVE

ALL AROUND ME, THE MIST SWIRLED. I WASN'T SURE WHERE I was, but I was in a long hallway that had red velvet wallpaper on the side, with dark wainscoting along the lower third of the wall. The end of the hallway seemed a long ways away—it seemed to telescope forward. I felt like I was drugged. Something had knocked me out, and now I had no clue what had happened to bring me to this place.

All right, I thought. *What's the last thing you can remember?*

All I could see was my car, with me standing next to it. Everything beyond that was blank. I remembered snow on the ground, and I remembered pulling into the driveway, but I couldn't remember where I'd been, or what happened after that.

Who am I? Do I know? seemed the next logical question.

January Jaxson, married to Killian O'Connell. Mother to Xi and Klaus, the cutest kittens ever born. So, that was something.

I looked around. *Where am I and how did I get here?*

I was in a house, it seemed. Even though the hallway telescoped out, I could feel the wallpaper under my fingers as I ran my hand along the wainscoting rail. The air smelled musty and old, as though nobody had been through here in a long, long time. To my right, a small room sat off the hallway. It was more like an alcove than a room. There were no doors to close it off.

Not sure what to do next, I walked into the alcove. There were two chairs there, with heart-shaped red leather backs and black upholstered seats, and they flanked a small round table with a marble top. The wood on both the chairs and table looked like pecan, with a rich orange undertone. The table held a lamp—one of those old Victorian ones that had been popular when I was a little girl. The rounded bottom and the top section had a scalloped top that surrounded the chimney. Both bottom and top were white, painted with tea roses, and crystals hung from a thin circle of metal, on which the top rested. I reached out and touched it, seeing no cords, and the bulb inside flickered on as my fingertips brushed the glass.

I sat there, trying to figure out if I was here to meet anyone.

Everything felt odd and out of place. I was in what appeared to be someone's home, yet the energy around me felt startlingly empty. As I wondered what to do next, I noticed a strange smell creeping around the edges.

It was familiar, and yet—it wasn't.

Another conundrum.

If I started to explore the hallway, opening doors to the other rooms along the way, I might intrude on somebody. And yet, whoever had invited me here was remiss in that they hadn't greeted me or made themselves known.

Wait, I thought. *How did I get on this floor? Where's the entrance to the house and the front door?*

More curious than ever, I stood and returned to the hallway, looking to my left. The hallway continued. However, the end of it didn't seem to telescope out like it did to the right, and I thought I could see a staircase at the end. Deciding to take a chance, I headed in that direction.

I set my focus on reaching the stairs, but at that moment, I realized that I was dressed in clothes that weren't mine. I was wearing a floor-length dress. It was snug, with a corset top and a peplum. The skirt was almost mermaid in style, with an actual *bustle*, and it narrowly followed the curve of my hips and legs to below my knees, where it splayed out. It was a two-piece outfit, a skirt and the corset-jacket. The sleeves poofed out around my upper arms, like mutton sleeves, fastened to the corset top at the point where my arms separated from my shoulders. They snugged in when they reached my elbows, and ended in pointed sleeves that covered the tops of my hands. The belt around my waist was a thin, black leather belt with silver fittings.

The material of the skirt and dress reminded me of upholstery, in both weight and texture. A pale mauve with ivory and gold flowers, it looked like the material that had covered my aunt Teran's sofa when I was young.

Very Laura Ashley, I thought.

I was also wearing a hat precariously perched on the top of my hair—which was gathered up into a high chignon—and I realized that I was carrying a parasol.

How the hell had I ended up dressed like someone out of a *Downton Abbey* episode? Or whatever time period this getup was from? I knew these weren't my regular clothes, so where did they come from? Was I in some fever dream?

"What's going on?" I startled myself with the sound of my voice. The air felt so muffled that I was surprised when the words reverberated through the hall.

"Is anybody here?" I asked. "Can anyone hear me?"

But as I neared the steps, they began to fade away as the left hall suddenly telescoped out, stretching to a point where I could barely see the end. The steps were now toward the new end, but it would take awhile to walk there. At first, it had seemed perfectly normal for me to be here, but now I realized that I was out of place, and I was out of phase.

"Who's responsible for this?" And then a thought occurred to me. "Am I dreaming? Am I hallucinating the entire thing? But I can feel the wall," I whispered, once again reaching out to touch the surface. "What the hell is happening? And why can't I find anybody?"

If I was in a real place, I should be able to find someone nearby.

"Hello? Is anybody here?" I called out. "Can anybody hear me?" But no one answered. Now I was spooked. Not only was I alone, but I seemed to be trapped.

All right. If I couldn't leave by the stairs, then I'd start opening doors. I began to breathe shallowly, and I realized that I was headed for a panic attack.

Calm down, you don't seem to be in any immediate danger. Figure out where you are, if you can. Search the other rooms.

I turned to the right and began to follow the hall. As I came to the next door—which was on my left—I reached for the handle. It was warm, very warm, and I questioned whether I should open the door, but finally decided to crack it. As I did, I heard the sizzle of flames, and before I could even see inside, I slammed the door.

"Good gods, is the house on fire?" My panic increased. I glanced at the bottom of the door, but no smoke drifted out from beneath it. I put my hand against the door itself. The wood was cool, but the handle felt hot.

Curious now, though still on high alert, I knelt and peeked through the keyhole.

I caught a glimpse of bright white-orange light inside the room. It was beautiful and radiant, and I could hear the crackle of flames. Yet I couldn't smell anything—fire or smoke—so I backed away from the door, shaking my head, then turned and ran down the hall to the next door, which was on the right. As I took hold of the handle, it felt cooler than the metal should.

Standing behind the door, I eased it open a crack, not wanting to be in the direct aim of anything or anyone that might be inside.

The moment I cracked the door, a howl of winds came rushing out, moaning and shrieking and rattling the light fixtures on the walls of the hallway. The sconces rattled, threatening to pull away from the walls. I peeked around the door, startled to see brilliant sky. Pale blue like early morning, billowing clouds raced across it. I couldn't see any floor, merely a long drop into the endless blue, and the winds tugged at me, trying to sweep me in. I managed to pull myself around to the back side of the door and slammed it, leaning against it as I breathed in the massive influx of clear, clean air.

A thought began to form in my mind. Fire...and sky... would the next door be a churning ocean, and the next a massive mountain? Was I in some magical nexus that offered entrance into the elemental realms? It wasn't out of the realm of possibility.

Curious, I began to count the doors. There were four primary elements, and as far as we knew, six sub-elements when it came to magic. Earth, air, fire, and water, then ice, lightning, mud, dust, lava, and steam. I counted the doors along the hall. Other than the alcove, which wasn't behind a door, I counted thirteen, including the room at the end of the hallway. So that meant three more realms than I had counted.

But though I was able to reach the end two doors, the door in front of me—at the very end of the hall—still tele-scoped outward. What was it? Where did it lead? Home, perhaps? But something told me, as I watched the door, that it wasn't a safe shortcut back to my house.

"What is this?" I asked, leaning back against the wall. I wanted to get out of here, to find my way back home, but at least now I knew why I hadn't met anybody. Or maybe there were others here, but I couldn't see them or hear them.

Then another thought struck me. Was I dead? Did I somehow end up here by mistake because I was too unaware to realize that I was dead?

But spirits wouldn't usually hang out around the elemental realms. Suppose, however, the spirit shamans weren't familiar with every type of spirit. Suppose I was a new kind. That wouldn't surprise me, given how I had always beat the odds in so many ways.

But...regardless of where I was, or how I got here, what should I do next?

Maybe Esmara could hear me? My great-aunt was one of our family's Ladies, who guided those of us in whom the witchblood was strong. They came to us when we were ready and helped guide us through life. It was worth a shot.

"Esmara, can you hear me? Esmara? I need you!" I paused, waiting. I usually was better at catching her attention when I spoke aloud. "Esmara, I need you!" Again, I waited. Again, nothing. I decided to try one more time. "Esmara? Can you hear me at all?"

Discouraged, I went back to the alcove and sat. I wanted out of here. I didn't want to go searching behind the other doors—especially if one of them happened to be lava.

Then I heard a click come from the silent hallway. I peeked around the corner to see if there was anybody there, but a sudden rush of dizziness hit me and I grabbed the table as I went reeling back into my chair. There was somebody near me, all right, and whoever it was, they were powerful.

"Esma—"

A laugh, low and malign, caught me off guard. I scrambled out of the chair as a shadow filled the room. It was huge and overpowering, like a thunder cloud taking form in front of me. I gasped, trying to get around it, into the hall.

The shadow grew larger, blocking my way, and now it was the shape of a man, blacker than the darkest ink, blacker than the bottom of the ocean. The oiliness of the shadow man oozed from every inch of his form.

"Who are you?" I backed up, into a corner, terrified.

You remember me, he said, stretching up and out to fill the room.

"No—no, I don't—" But even as I protested, a part of me did.

Flash... I was young, too young to make sense of the world, and I was in my toddler bed, alone. Aunt Teran was there, somewhere, but I was supposed to go to sleep.

Flash... As she turned the light off and left the room, it was darker than it was supposed to be, and a looming presence filled the room. Whatever it was scared the hell out of me and I pulled my blanket up around my chest as I sat up and tried to look around the room.

Flash... I began to cry. Someone was there, someone who meant to harm me. I could feel him nearby, and there was nothing I could do. Mama and Papa weren't around. Aunt Teran was in the other room. And I was alone with a dark, powerful creature.

Flash... I screwed up my face and begin to whimper, scooting back against the headboard of my bed. I cowered under my blanket as two glowing eyes appeared in the inky blackness of his face. The shadow moved toward me, and I let out a screech loud enough to wake the dead.

Flash... The shadow man loomed over me, reaching out with a long, jointed finger made of black smoke. He swiped across my forehead, scratching me. As the blood welled up, I screamed. The murky energy coiled around me, like a snake constricting its prey, and I gasped, trying to breathe. At that moment, Teran slammed the door open and lunged forward, my mother's dagger in hand.

"Leave her alone! I banish thee to the darkest realms of hell, you motherfucker!" She struck the tip of the blade into the middle of the shadow, murmuring some incantation, and the shadow man burst into a puff of smoke and ash, loosening his grip on me as he vanished.

Aunt Teran gathered me into her arms, tears trailing down her cheeks. "Oh, child. I'm so sorry." She kissed my tears, then examined me as I continued to cry. "Oh great mother, you're wearing his mark. I have to protect you. I have to do something to prevent him from coming back. Your mother won't..." She paused, then whispered, "Never mind. I'll take care of what needs to be done. Your mother doesn't have to know."

I didn't understand what she was saying. All I knew was my aunt had come to my rescue and I wasn't alone. She hugged me until my tears dried. After I calmed down, she created a circle of strength and protection. The dark shadow creature was still near, I could tell. Aunt Teran sat me in the center of the circle and she sprinkled me with some sort of water, and drew a pentacle on my forehead. Then, as she spoke, I began to close my eyes as a cozy energy surrounded me, like sunshine on a summer's day. The shadow man vanished, and as I drifted off to sleep, all I knew was that Aunt Teran had saved me.

I STRAIGHTENED AS THE SHADOW MAN CONTINUED TO approach. "You cannot touch me," I said, holding up my hand. "I wear the mark of Druantia, protected by her blessings, and I walk under her guidance."

"Don't be so sure. Not all gods can travel to the space where you now stand. I've been waiting for you." His words echoed around me. I had the feeling he wanted something beyond my energy.

"What do you want?" I asked, stalling for time so I could figure out what to do.

"You burn too brightly. You impede the darkness."

I wasn't sure what he meant by that, but whatever the case, his intentions were far from good. This was definitely the same shadow man I'd seen when I was a child. He had marked me and followed me all through my life.

Nobody was quite sure what the race of shadow people actually were. We knew they were energy vampires, and we knew they could kill, and they could affect the behavior of mortals. But as to their agenda, it was hidden behind the veil of smoke and ash.

I closed my eyes and thought of Druantia, the goddess to whom Teran had bound me that fateful night. I hadn't known about it, not until a few years ago, but when I found out and sought the earth goddess out, I had decided to re-up my pledge to her as an adult. She had accepted me.

By the power of three times three,
By the powers of earth the mighty,
By the powers of crystal and bone,
By the powers of tree and stone,
I cast thee out from this space,
Begone, you creature of vile race.

As I conjured the incantation, I focused on drawing my power up from the earth, but it was hard to find the thread.

The house I was in wasn't a *house*—at least not in the physical realm I was used to inhabiting.

Then I thought about the elemental doors. If I could find the door leading into the elemental realm of earth, I might be able to tap into the purest energy from that element. Druantia was a goddess of the earth, a goddess of the planet itself. And when I'd met the Aseer, she had assessed me as strong in the element of Earth, and in the realm of spirits—working with the dead.

There was a narrow space between the shadow man and the wall. Trying to avoid giving away my intention, I darted through that space, racing for the archway of the alcove. I turned right and began running down the hall. I remembered the door leading to fire and air, and I took a chance that the next door might be earth. I yanked it open, leaping back as a cascade of water crested against the barrier keeping the element within. I slammed the door and ran to the next one.

As I pulled it open, I could see the shadow man chasing me. He'd be on me in seconds. I prayed I was right and faced the open door.

There, inside, was the land. Solid land with grass up to my knees. Trees dappled the landscape, as did massive crystals jutting out of the ground, and everywhere, bones rose out of the ground, bones of humanoids, bones of animals, bones of creatures I could only guess the nature of.

"Druantia, give me strength!" I felt the power of earth come rushing to embrace me. *Like recognizes like*, I thought. And the element of earth was my element.

I am here. The goddess's words echoed through the air, through my heart. Druantia surrounded me, buoying me up. She washed through me like a summer evening as the air began to cool. The scent of lilacs and cedar washed through my lungs.

Dragonflies on the wing, and birds singing their mystical night songs... The rustle of animals in the forest, prowling and on the hunt... The scent of old bones, dry with age but rich with history... The strength of the world spinning on its axis as history wore on and on, passing like a stream through the night... The magic of dryads and gnomes and kobolds and trolls...

All these energies collected in my heart, radiating through my body, enclosing me in armor so strong it would break any weapon used against it. The armor of earth, forged in the core of the world, forged from liquid rock and ore, surrounded me.

I turned to the shadow man who was now standing in front of me. He could not touch me, not in this moment. He could do nothing save stare at me, frustrated.

I whispered, "Druantia, can you take me home?"

I couldn't fight him—not without understanding how his kind worked, but I could hopefully remove myself from the situation before he could hurt me.

I can. Close your eyes and ride the dragon.

I closed my eyes and, sure enough, there was a dark green dragon sitting there, waiting for me. He was young, the size of a horse, with golden topaz eyes and emerald pupils. I walked over and climbed aboard his back. Suddenly, the Victorian dress was gone, and I was clad in what looked like leather. The dragon waited patiently, and when I was settled, he gestured to me with his head, his eyes beginning to spin.

I took a deep breath, and we began to move. The house fell away from us, dropping into oblivion, and we were flying through space. The stars had never sparkled in such a dazzling array and I tried not to cry out when I found myself facing a million stars, a thousand galaxies.

Are we on the Milky Way? I asked.

We are, the dragon answered. *Now sleep.*

And I closed my eyes and fell asleep on the back of the dragon.

CHAPTER SIX

"JANUARY? CAN YOU HEAR ME?" THE VOICE WAS SOFT, echoing in my ears. I squinted, opening one eye, to see Killian sitting beside me on his side of the bed. Standing to my left was Dr. Fairsight.

"She's coming around," the doctor said. She leaned over and felt my forehead. "The fever seems to have broken."

"What...?" I could barely get the word out, my throat felt so parched. "Water?"

"In a moment. I want to check you out. You've been a very sick woman, and I need to make certain you're okay." She settled beside me, brushing back my hair. She scanned a thermometer at my forehead. "Your fever's down to 101 degrees. Good, that's a relief. Now, can you handle it if I point a light at your eyes? You tell me if it hurts too much."

She brought up a pen light and flashed it toward my eyes. The light hurt, but it didn't knock me for a loop. I grunted, but tried to keep my eyes open. "Is this okay?" she asked.

Nodding, I said in a crackly voice, "Yeah, I can manage. What happened? What time is it?"

The doctor put away her light and held up her hand. "How many fingers do you see?"

"Three," I answered. "What happened?"

She took my pulse and held it for a moment, then wrapped a blood pressure cuff around my upper arm. When she had finished and marked her findings down on the chart, she let out a sigh. "Okay, you seem to be on the mend. We'll answer your questions in good time, but first, I'll give you a drink, but we also have you hooked up to an IV for fluids."

I glanced up at the head of the bed, where an IV pole stood, holding a bag of clear liquid. The tube ran down to a needle that was taped across my arm. "What the...what happened?"

"That's a mixture of fluids and electrolytes. You're dehydrated. Your temperature was so high we almost took you to the hospital. You were up to 105 degrees, my girl." She took a compress off my head and replaced it with another, cooler one.

"Oh, love, I was so worried," Killian said. "Teran called me at work after she called the doctor."

"Teran? Where is she? I..." The last thing I remembered was Druantia, and the shadow man. *The shadow man!* I struggled to sit up. "I need to talk to her—"

"I'm right here." My aunt walked over beside the doctor. "You became agitated and you were flushed. I felt your forehead and you were burning up, so I called the doctor, and then Killian." She turned to the doctor. "Do you know what it might be? Does she have a virus?"

"I don't think so," the doctor said.

"No, it's not that. I'm not sick." Once again, I struggled to sit up. "Aunt Teran, it was the shadow man."

Teran froze, her eyes widening. "What did you say?"

"The shadow man—I saw him again. The same one as

when I was little." I finally made them help me sit up against the pillows.

The doctor checked my temperature again and it was already back to normal. She insisted on keeping me hooked up to the fluids but gave me a glass of water to go with it.

"You had an encounter with a shadow man?" Dr. Linda Fairsight specialized in treating Otherkin, and she knew all about the outer realms.

I nodded. "When I was a toddler, one almost got me. He marked me, but Aunt Teran chased him off. But I was in this...wait..." Images began to flicker in and out. "I was in a house. I recognize it from somewhere before, but I can't quite pinpoint it. But I was there, and...there were doors to the elements, and another door. The shadow man came out of the twelfth door, and he was trying to latch on to me. He remembered me, and I flashed back to when I was in my bed and Aunt Teran protected me from him. I managed to hook into the earth element energy, and Druantia helped me get out of there. That's when I woke up. I remember opening a door to the fire element. Could that be where my fever came from?"

"It could be," the doctor said. "I couldn't find any pathological reason for it, and when the fever began to decrease, you began to come around. You do know that, even though they're from the Void, shadow people are often connected with the realm of fire? They drain energy and it somehow drains moisture, as well. If he was latching onto you, that could have been what caused the intense and sudden dehydration."

"Is he still fastened into you?" Killian asked. The low, gruff voice coming out of my husband was his protective mode. If he could go full wolf on the shadow man, he would.

"No," I said. "I managed to erect a barrier using the earth energy."

Are you all right? Oh, my darling... Esmara walked through the wall, looking frantic. *I heard you call but couldn't get away. What happened? Where were you?*

I let the others know Esmara had joined us and began telling everyone what had happened. I took it one step at a time, describing everything I could remember. "As I said, the place I was in—I know it from *somewhere*, but I can't figure out where."

"Well, one thing's certain. The shadow man is on the prowl again. I wonder what woke him up."

"Tell me more about shadow people," Killian said. "I don't know much."

"They latch onto one person at a time and often follow that person through their life, like a parasitic leech. Sometimes they drain them dry and the person will die, but other times they keep a steady pace, and the person will suffer from chronic fatigue or illness. There are medical reasons for chronic fatigue, of course, but there have been some—especially among Otherkin, or humans with a high psychic ability—where the continuous drain siphons off the energy needed to function on a normal basis."

"Could he be causing January's ERS?" Killian asked.

I shook my head. "I don't think so—"

"Energy reflux syndrome is almost always caused by a backlog of magical energy that hasn't been used. It creates a blockage—think of it like a plug or a clog. The regular use of magic keeps the pipes clean. So no, I don't think he's to blame for January's ERS," the doctor said.

"But he's still attached to her?"

"Now that I know what to look for, I can see both his mark, and the mark Druantia gave her." The doctor sat back in her chair, contemplating my file. "The shadow man still has his hooks lodged in her, though right now he can't drain her energy. Since there's almost no way to dislodge him other than to destroy him, he'll continue to look for a way in and another opportunity to strike. January has a tremendous amount of magical energy, especially since it's all gunked up inside, and that alone is enough to attract a shadow person."

"How do we destroy him?" Killian asked.

"While you can send them back to their realm from here, you have to destroy them either in a nexus, or their realm. And you must use light as a weapon. Shadow people are the antithesis of light, and it will shatter them, like too much darkness can shatter light. Every person carries a balance within. When the shadow side grows too strong, their acts become shadowed. When the light grows too bright, they burn rather than help."

"It always comes down to the balance," I said. "The balance is everything."

You are right, my dear. The balance keeps us from growing too self-righteous, or too malign. Opposite sides of the same coin, and all too likely to result in destruction either way. Esmara walked over to the bed. *You said you were in a house? An old Victorian?*

I nodded. "Yes, I was." I told the others Esmara was asking me questions.

"I have to leave," the doctor said. "I have another house call to make. You should be all right now. I'll unhook the IV for now, but make certain you drink at least four or five glasses of water after I leave—tonight, not over the next few days. Hydrate yourself. If the fever returns, call me." She stood, sliding my file into her briefcase. And with that, Dr. Fairsight left for the evening, and Killian went in the kitchen to fix me some soup and toast for dinner.

Teran took off her shoes and scooted onto the bed, sitting against the headboard next to me. "So, how are you, really?"

I started to say I was fine, but then stopped. She knew me better than I knew myself.

"Scared. And wondering—what was the place I was in? I've been there before, but I don't remember when. It reminded me of some dream. What do you know about shadow people? You were there that night. Why did he come for me?"

"You were close by and you were a bright beacon of energy. He was hungry. I'd say it was as simple as that," she said. "Shadow people... What we don't know about them would fill a book. They aren't spirits—as in ghosts. They don't operate under the same rules. They're almost always evil. Basically, they're a form of energy vampire. Predators. They don't discriminate with who they attack. Adult, child...it doesn't matter to them. They feed on both fear and on energy."

The lights seemed to flicker. "How long have they been around?"

"Since the dawn of life, I imagine. They've been mentioned down through history in one form or another. Change the wording, change the country or culture, but they're always there. They're a lot more common than you want to think. My best guess is that their world intersects with ours via portals, and it sounds like you were in a nexus point—a place where many worlds collide."

She looked up as Killian carried in a bed tray with two bowls of soup and toast.

"I thought you might like a bite to eat, too. Chicken and rice soup okay?"

"Chicken and rice is fine. You are the dearest boy," Teran said.

I suppressed a snort. Killian was almost twice as old as Teran, but he was far younger in nature. "He's the best husband ever!" Wincing—my overenthusiastic reply actually made my head hurt—I picked up a piece of toast.

"You're right. If I was ever interested in marrying, I'd want someone like Killian, age appropriate."

He laughed. "I'm at least fifty years older than you, Teran. Age is a state of mind." He sat down in the chair near the bed. "So, why haven't you ever wanted to marry, if I'm not being too personal?"

"I think you know that I was engaged once, but Rowan proved the man was a cad. It tore us apart for a while, but I'm grateful she did what she did." Teran sighed. "You know that my mother left her inheritance to January because I didn't produce a grandchild."

"I wonder if she believed I was planning on having kids, because she would have been sorely disappointed had I told her the truth," I murmured. Nonny had been strict and her outlook, black and white.

Teran shrugged. "It doesn't matter now. By the way, the lawyers are setting up an appointment for us. I still can't believe you're giving me her estate in Ireland. But you have to drive out and look at the cabin. It's perfect for the two of you, and I'm more comfortable in town."

"Thank you," I whispered. "I couldn't leave you out of this." I leaned my head on her shoulder. "How could I take her entire estate while you sat out in the cold? Nonny was cruel, in some ways."

Teran kissed my forehead. "You're one hell of a niece. My life would be empty without you." She turned to Killian. "When I was growing up, I always felt on the outside of relationships. I never felt like I truly belonged to any particular group. I'm not asexual, but neither was I focused on boys, or girls, or anything like that. I enjoyed my friendships but I didn't like sharing my space. When I finally did start dating, I hated the time that girls put into picking out the right clothes and going over what they should say. That alone served to make me pretty unpopular."

Killian leaned back, nodding. He thought for a moment, then said, "You were a freethinker."

"I was a free *spirit*. People think I'm a holdover from the hippie era, but I was always too ambitious for that mindset. I make my own way, do my own thing, and if someone wants to walk beside me for a while, that's cool. But I'm not here to coddle, and I'm not here to shore up somebody else." She paused, worrying her lip.

"What is it?" I asked.

"I've never told you this...I didn't want you to think ill of your mother, but it helps explain my choices." She raised her gaze to mine.

"Go on," I said.

"When Althea and I were in our teens, something happened. Something your mother never told anyone about. I was the only one who knew."

My stomach knotted. I could tell that whatever she was about to say, it wasn't good.

"Your mother was sixteen and I was twelve. She wanted to sneak out on a date one night and I helped her. Our parents were strict about boys. They wanted to meet the boy first, and only after they vetted him would we be allowed to date. This particular boy was named Jorden. He was gorgeous— glam rock hair, shirts open to his navel, you get the idea. And Althea was absolutely bewitched."

"Let me guess—Nonny refused to let them date?"

"Nonny didn't even *know* about him. Our mother would have forbidden Althea to date him—he was an asshole, for one thing, and he was stupid, for another. But he was glorious to look at, and at that time, Althea's hormones were running wild. I helped her sneak out, even though I thought she was making a big mistake. She came home late, and I had to cover for her. At one in the morning, she climbed up the trellis, in through the window."

Something was coming, though I didn't know what. "Did your parents find out?"

"No," Teran said. "I thought about telling them, but your mother begged me not to. When she came through the window, the first thing I noticed was that her skirt and shirt were torn. She was covered with grass stains. I hustled her in. Althea was crying, and her knees and hands were scraped. Turns out Jorden had taken her to his friend's house, where there were three other guys waiting. They tried to rape your mother—"

"Oh my gods..." I stared at Teran.

"They found out why it isn't wise to attack a witch. She blew up the house, basically. Two of the boys were injured—one with a broken pelvis, and the other had second-degree burns. Jorden ended up with both ankles broken, a broken jaw, and a broken clavicle. Your mother escaped before they could get their hands on her, but the force of her power terrified her. Even though it was totally defensive, she stopped working anything but simple magic that night. The next day, the reports were that the furnace blew, destroying most of the house and contents. Nobody was killed, and insurance paid for it, but your mother and I knew the truth. And so did those three boys, but they never said a word. How could they?"

"So that was another reason my mother feared magic. Because of how powerful she was."

"How powerful she could have *been*. She shut down. She seldom ever used her magic after that, even though she went through the motions. Oh, she read cards, she told fortunes, and mixed up cookies with magic sprinkled in them. But at heart, she was terrified of her potential. That's why she refused to join the Crystal Cauldron."

"And she was afraid of my potential, and of the curse, and the combination led her to ignore my training."

"Right." Teran sat back, shaking her head. "When she came home that night, I swore no man would ever have a chance to make me fear my power. Nor would I allow anyone to make me bury my power like that to survive."

"Until Caine," I said.

"Even then, I held a part of myself in reserve. And when Rowan proved him to be a liar, I walked away. I cried, yes, but he furthered my views that I was meant to live an independent life."

"Whatever happened to Jorden?" Killian asked.

"He died in a drunken car crash a few years later. He and his buddies—the same ones that attacked your mother—drank a bottle of tequila and tried to take a curve near the bay at over a hundred miles an hour. They went into the water and were too drunk to escape from the car. They drowned." She smiled softly. "Your mother, when she found out, merely changed the subject."

As we settled into eating our soup, Killian turned on the TV to a nature documentary and lowered the sound to a manageable level.

I thought about my mother. I wished I had more time with her. But really, I wished I had left Ellison a lot earlier and spent more time with my family. I let him come between me and my friendships, and me and my relatives. With a warmth in my heart I glanced at Killian. Ellison would have been rude to Teran and hustled her out. But Killian opened his home—our home—and his heart to her. And that meant all the world to me.

CHAPTER SEVEN

I MUST HAVE FALLEN ASLEEP AGAIN, BECAUSE WHEN I WOKE it was morning and Teran was gone.

The clock on my phone read eight A.M. I threw back the covers, pausing as I braced for impact. But the dizziness was gone, as were the hammers beating a rhythm in my brain. After giving myself the go-ahead, I slipped out of bed and padded into the bath to take a shower. I lathered up with vanilla-lilac body wash, then after a thorough rinse, I dried off and shook my hair out of the bathing cap. I'd wash it later.

I chose a warm but comfortable outfit—a burgundy skirt that ended below my knees, a fitted mauve sweater with a sweetheart neckline and long sleeves, and knee-high black leather boots. I brushed my hair back, slipped on a satin headband, and then added the gold and emerald necklace that had belonged to my great-great grandmother Ellen, a powerful witch who lived in Ireland. We had determined that it was, indeed, enchanted, though it only boosted feelings of self-confidence and self-esteem. As mild as the magic was, it helped me after one of my migraines.

I fastened on a pair of gold hoop earrings that matched

the necklace, and then headed for the kitchen. The table was high with a pile of gifts. My presents, from my birthday party.

"I almost forgot about these," I said, stopping by the mound on the table. "I'll go through them this evening."

Killian looked delighted to see me up and around. "You good enough to be on your feet?" He held out a plate with toast on it. I saw that he had scrambled some eggs as well.

I grabbed a piece and then leaned in for a kiss. His lips were warm against my own and I murmured a soft "Miss you" as I nibbled on them. But he had a busy day, and I didn't trust the lack of headache to continue, so instead of pursuing the direction my mind was running, I added some eggs to a plate and a second piece of toast, as well as a bowl of fruit salad, then sat down at the kitchen table.

"I miss you too, by the way," Killian said. "But this morning..."

"I know, we're both busy. More's the pity. But at least I'm on my feet and feeling pretty good. Those new drugs the doctor has me on sure help me recover faster." I bit into my toast, then wiped my hands on a napkin. "It sucks that I missed part of my birthday, but the party at work was wonderful. Thank you, love."

"I know you aren't fond of surprises, but I thought you wouldn't mind that one."

"When did Teran go home? Did she stay the night?"

"No, she went home shortly after you fell asleep. She said for you to call her when you get the chance." Killian kissed me again. "I'll see you this evening. If the migraine returns, let me know. Okay?"

"All right," I murmured, then waved as he headed out. I texted Tad that I might be in during the afternoon, and that I'd let him know for sure by noon. He sent back a thumbs-up.

After making sure Killian had fed the cats, I walked over to the window and stared outside. Ari was at work; I could see her car in the driveway. I wanted to talk to her, but I couldn't interrupt her appointments. Instead, I pulled out my phone and called Rowan.

"What's up, girl?" my grandmother asked.

"I need to talk. About the shadow man."

"Teran called me this morning to tell me what happened, but it would be best if you told me yourself, in case she left out any details. Let me get a pen and paper so I can take notes."

As I waited, I sorted through the details to make certain I remembered them as accurately as I could. When Rowan returned, I told her everything that had happened from the moment after the party until I woke up in bed.

"It sounds like you were in a portal house," she said.

"What's that?" I'd heard of portals, but never portal houses.

"A portal house is a nexus. Other creatures and entities might see it as something different, but in every case I've heard of, if the being is from our world—Otherkin, human, whatever—they have seen it as a house. It might be a shrine or a temple to someone from Japan, or a large series of huts to someone from another culture, or—in your case, an old Victorian—but no matter how it presents, it's a conduit to other realms. It seems you happened to stumble into a nexus leading to the elements."

"But it also had a door to the shadow realm? I didn't think the shadow realm was an elemental realm." I was confused.

"It is, and it isn't. I'm surprised you didn't also find a door to the realm of light, although it was probably behind one of the other two doors—and I'll wager the netherworld was behind the end door. Light beings tend to be more reclusive than the shadow people." Rowan was frowning—I could hear it in her voice. "You say you made it into the realm of earth and used that energy to protect yourself?"

"Yes, I called on Druantia while I was there and she sent me home on a dragon."

"Well, that's handy," Rowan said.

"It was different, I'll say that much. I have no idea if it was a dragon, or if it was something else in a form that I'd recognize. Wait," I said, suddenly realizing what she had said. "You mean there's a realm of *light*, like there is shadow?"

"Yes, there is, and make no mistake, the beings from that realm can kill you as easily as the shadow people. I don't think they *intend* to do so, but they're so blindingly strong in their energy that it sort of...burns. Shadow people drain others. The light beings overload them with power. They seem oblivious to us, to be honest. I don't know if they can see anything beyond their own brilliance. It's not narcissism, either. They simply cannot see beyond the blinding light of their existence. It's like standing next to a sun—the sun doesn't *mean* to incinerate you, but that's what happens."

I took a deep breath. "If I had opened a door into the realm of light..."

"You remember how strong the fire was, when you opened its gateway?"

"Right. And if I exposed myself to the light, I wouldn't be here, would I?" The enormity of what could have happened slammed home.

"You would have died. The strength of the light would have instantly incinerated the cord to your body and sent you cartwheeling off to your Ladies. The shadow people take longer to kill others." She sighed. "Which is why the light beings are far more dangerous. I don't recall any stories of someone taking them on and winning. On the other hand, they don't hook into humans and act as leeches, either."

"Okay then. But Rowan, how the hell did I get out there in the first place? And why did it feel so familiar?"

"Have you tried any new magic lately? Or picked up any

new magical tools? Sometimes you can bring home something tied to the nexus realms."

"I don't think so. No on the magic. And as far as buying new tools, I haven't done that either." I froze. "Wait. I think... Can you come over right away? I think I might know what triggered it, but I want somebody here when I check it out. I don't want to get cast out there again." I glanced at the pile of presents. One present there didn't fit into the mix.

"I'll be over in half an hour. Don't do anything till I get there." Rowan hung up.

I cautiously approached the table. There, to one side, was the mirror. I didn't let myself look into it, but skirted around the edge of the table, feeling the hairs on the back of my neck stand up. I glanced over my shoulder. There was no one there, but I knew that the house wasn't empty. I was here, the cats were here, and it slowly dawned on me that we weren't alone.

"Esmara? Esmara, I need you!" I didn't want to be alone until Rowan arrived.

PLEASE, COME AS FAST AS YOU CAN. I CAN FEEL SOMETHING IN THE HOUSE WITH ME, I texted her.

Are you all right, child? Esmara popped in next to me.

I jumped, my hand on my heart. "You scared the crap out of me!"

What's going on? There's someone here—and I don't think they're friendly. Esmara motioned for me to sit down.

Xi and Klaus chose that moment to come bounding into the kitchen, where they leapt on the chair next to me, vying for footing.

Dark... We're scared, Xi projected to me. She was my familiar, and we had been developing a rudimentary connection, thought-wise, since she had grown up.

"I know, little one. Stay here with me." I grabbed a large kitchen knife from the block. When in need, improvise! I held it out and began to draw a tight circle around the cats and me.

Maiden, Mother, Crone of Darkest Night,
Weave now, this Circle tight,
From bones and breath, from flames and tears,
Bring protection, cast out fear.
From earth and air, from fire and water,
Heed me now, Earth's witchblood daughter!

As the energy settled around us in a resounding ring, Esmara poured her own energy into it, strengthening the circle of protection. She joined us inside the circle as I picked up Klaus. Xi was smart enough to stay here on her own, but I wasn't so sure about my fuzzy boy.

But Xi let out a few mews and he jumped down, curling up beneath the chair.

"Can you make him stay in the circle?" I asked.

He'll stay with us, was all Xi said. But her thoughts were certain, reassuring me.

Esmara pointed to the pile of gifts. *It's coming from that mirror. Whatever is focused on us, it is trying to break through.*

"I know," I said. "I don't know what to do, but Rowan's on the way."

Rowan's strong enough to help drive him back, if she gets here before he breaks through.

"Can he hurt you?" I hoped not, because if he could, that meant he could destroy the Ladies. And that would be very, very bad for my family.

Yes, the shadow people can target spirits as well as mortals. Which is why I'm staying here in this circle. I think we've made it strong enough to repel him—

Esmara stopped as the mirror began to rattle. It was sitting on the table, and now, it began to shake and thump against the surface. It wasn't strong enough to break the glass, but it was scary enough to watch. It levitated, then dropped several times.

"What's it trying to do?" I asked.

I'm not sure, but if I had to guess, I'd say something's trying to get through.

"Crap, I thought he was already through." Then I realized he *was*. He was already in the house. He didn't necessarily need the mirror. So if it wasn't him, what was trying to break through? And what the hell was strong enough to slam the mirror up and down?

At that moment, someone knocked on the kitchen door and it swung open. Ari was standing there, and the moment she opened the door, her eyes went wide and she gasped.

"Shut the door—get out!" I said, but it was too late.

A bolt of energy shot out of the mirror and slammed into Ari, hitting her directly in the chest. She staggered back, as though she'd been shot.

"Ari!" I jumped up and—ignoring the circle—raced to her side.

She sprawled on the ground, convulsing.

A loud laugh rang out and I looked up in time to see a dark shadow looming over me. *The shadow man.* As he reached for me, I rolled out of the way, trying to shove Ari to the side. I scrambled to remember banishing spells that didn't require setting up in advance, but my mind was still slow, and I was so startled by what had happened that I wasn't thinking straight. But I was clear enough to hear Rowan's car pull in. I let out a scream, to let her know that something was wrong.

Meanwhile, I could see Esmara in the circle, Xi and Klaus huddling at her feet. Esmara was staring at Ari, full-blown horror on her face.

I managed to get on my feet as the shadow man turned to me and reached out again.

Dark as night, dark as blight,
I drive thee back, out of my sight!

I sent a massive wave of energy toward the shadow man and he stumbled back. I focused on strengthening that wave and could feel Esmara pouring energy into me from within the circle. I caught hold of it, adding her power to mine, and turned it full onto the shadow man.

As Rowan appeared at the door, the shadow man turned and fled, vanishing from the kitchen. Rowan took one look at Ari and knelt by her side. "What the hell is going on?"

"Something slammed into—"

Ari interrupted, smoothly sitting up. Her eyes had turned bright red, and she let out an echoing laughter, sounding deep as the world's core. "Get away from me, Old Crone," she snarled. She paused, then darted past Rowan, out of the door.

I immediately grabbed my phone and called Donna, the nanny. "Donna, lock the doors now. Don't let Ari inside, whatever you do! It's an emergency."

"What's going on?" Donna's voice quavered, but I could tell she was on the run. She knew enough about Ari and me to obey when one of us issued a direct order. "Okay, I locked the front door and the rest of the doors are locked already."

"Double check—make certain there's no way into the house."

"All right, hold on." A moment later she said, "All the doors are locked, but she's banging on the kitchen door. What the hell is happening?"

"I want you to take the kids and lock yourself in one of the rooms without a window. We'll be over in a moment. Do what I say. Ari's possessed." I turned to Rowan. "We have to stop her. We can't let her near the kids."

Rowan didn't stop to ask why, merely nodded, and put in a call to Tarvish. "Get your ass over here, now. We need you.

66

And bring the silver chains as well as the iron ones. Cuffs included. I have most of my spell kit here with me."

She looked back at me. "Come on. Esmara will stay with the cats." Rowan had been developing her sight and, with Esmara letting down her guard, Rowan could see her at times.

As we headed out the side door, I told Rowan what had happened. "I don't know what it is, but it's not the shadow man."

"It's a demon of some sort. It probably came through the mirror. Tarvish might be able to take it on—he's a demon."

"He's a Funtime demon, and he's not truly demonic." A thought hit me. "But I know someone who is. Do what you can—I'll be back in a moment." I began to race through the long backyard toward the Mystic Wood. I knew a real demon, and though she was considered a minor one, she might be able to help.

"Rebecca! Rebecca!" I started calling out when I was almost to the end of the yard. The Mystic Wood was shrouded in mist today. The snow was still sticking here, given how little sunlight fell through its canopy. My feet were freezing by now.

Sure enough, there she was—Rebecca. She watched me curiously, waiting till I arrived and dropped onto the bench next to the trailhead that led through the woodland. I leaned over, gasping. I wasn't used to sprints, and it was cold and humid. But after a moment, I caught hold of my breath and exhaled, long and slow.

"I need your help. A demon's loose, and it's possessing Ari. She's trying to get into the house now, and her kids are in there."

Rebecca narrowed her eyes. She was the perfect picture of a rosy-cheeked, golden-haired young girl, but behind that façade, she was an imp—a minor demon. When I was a child she had tried to kill me, but since I'd moved back, we'd become...not exactly friends, but cohorts.

"What are you talking about?"

"Somebody gave me a magic mirror, and something I think is a demon came out of it and possessed Ari. I don't have the time to waste. Can you help?"

Rebecca gazed up at the house. "It's been decades since I left the woodland. Only for you, January, would I set forth into the world. Only for you."

"And I have to live with that," I said. "All right, follow me."

I hesitated, then reached out my hand. She placed her small fingers in my palm, but the crackle upon touching her immediately dispelled any doubts that the girl in front of me was an illusion. I had no idea what the demon was doing to Ari, from the inside out. It could be frying her circuits, for all I knew.

Rebecca held tight and jogged along with me as we made our way back to the house. There stood Rowan in a standoff with Ari. I could feel the immense power from the demon as it sneered at my grandmother.

Letting go of my hand, Rebecca took a step forward. I gasped as the golden-haired girl dissolved, and there—in her place—stood a wide-eyed Fae-like creature that looked both youthful and dangerous. She now had almond-shaped eyes, large and on a slant, set wide on her face. Even though she was taller than me, she seemed somewhat ill-proportioned. In her natural state, Rebecca was beautiful and frightening and monstrous all at the same time. Her hair flowed over her shoulders, platinum striped with black, stark against the brilliant yellow eyes and bumblebee stripes of her clothes.

"Is that you?" I blurted out.

"Of course it's me," she said, her voice less melodic. She

turned toward Ari and narrowed her eyes. "This is my territory. Begone before I destroy you."

Ari stared at Rebecca. She no longer looked quite so confident, and I could sense hesitation under the surface.

Rebecca held out her hands. "*Don't make me send you packing.* You claim no territorial rights here, and these humans are under my protection."

That threw me. I'd never once heard Rebecca mention anything about territory or protecting us or anything of the sort. I wanted to ask her what she was talking about but had the feeling she could deal with whatever was possessing Ari better than I could, so I kept my mouth shut.

"You wouldn't dare—" Ari leaned forward, narrowing her eyes. But the uncertainty in her voice increased. "We're from the same source—"

"The hell we are. I'm a proper imp, you're an imposter. A *walk-in.* You steal your hosts, you're a scavenger, not a predator. You have to the count of four, or I'll blast you out of her body so fast you'll be on the other side of the world before you can blink." Rebecca cleared her throat. "One." She'd been eerie before, but now—in her natural shape and angry—she embodied the stuff of nightmares. "Two."

"All right, all right," Ari stumbled back. "I'm going." And, before Rebecca could say "Three," there was a flash and Ari slumped to the floor. A pillar of smoke shot out of her head and vanished into the sky.

Rebecca lifted her hand and shot a bolt of electrical green energy toward the center of the smoke, disrupting it. A shower of tiny black pebbles rained to the ground around us.

"All gone," she said, and in that moment, she shimmered back into the form I'd always known her by. "I'll take two sides of ribs, thank you. When you get around to it."

"I'll make it three," I murmured, settling down on the frozen steps next to Ari.

CHAPTER EIGHT

I helped Ari sit up as Rowan joined us.

Ari moaned as she leaned forward, trying to clear her head. "What happened? I feel like I got flattened by a truck." She rested her elbows on her knees. "Well, everything hurts, I can tell you that."

"Do you remember anything?" Rowan asked.

She shook her head. "No, not really." She looked around. "What's going on?"

Rebecca was still there. She approached us cautiously.

Ari stared at her. "You... I remember you were shouting at me—"

"Not at *you*. At the demon who was possessing you. I sent it away." Her voice was flowery innocence again, but now I knew that, beneath those rosy cheeks, lurked an incredibly powerful demon.

"Thank you," Ari said, then froze. "Oh hell, I shouldn't have said that, should I?"

"Demons aren't like the Overkings. They're the ones who will bind you for gratitude," Rebecca said, using the Mystic Wood term for the Fae.

"I already promised her ribs," I said. "We're good. And Rebecca, I truly appreciate what you did. I didn't expect it."

"Perhaps that's why I chose to come to your aid," she said, a gleam in her eye. "I'm off. Bring me the ribs this week."

"Will do," I said as she headed toward the backyard, returning to the Mystic Wood. "Well, I never expected *that*." I watched as she vanished around the corner of the house.

Rowan took Ari's hands and pulled her to her feet. "Let's go inside."

"Are you sure she's clear?" I asked.

"Yes, she is. Rebecca knocked the demon for a loop. She shattered it." Rowan helped Ari to the front door.

I followed but stopped when I saw Tarvish ease the car into the driveway. As he emerged from the car, I hurried over to ask him if he'd go check on the cats. I told him Esmara was watching over them in a circle, so he'd know she was there. "Tell her that Rebecca knocked the demon out of commission, but that the shadow man is probably still in the house, or around it. Say Esmara's name three times, and she should hear you."

"You sure you don't want me to call Beetlejuice instead?"

I laughed. "I needed that. Thanks, Big Guy."

Tarvis winked at me and lumbered over toward our house.

AS I ENTERED THE SALON—MY OLD HOUSE—FRIEDA, ARI'S assistant hair dresser, nodded at me. She was on the phone, rescheduling clients. Rowan was sitting by Ari in the kitchen, and Donna was there with the kids.

"Will it come back?" Ari asked, her breath short.

"No, Rebecca smashed it to smithereens. I had no clue she was that powerful. I mean, she tried to kill me when I was little, but now I'm wondering if that was true. She could have easily dragged me off into the woods. And I never saw her natural form. I wonder if she wanted something else, instead." If she had wanted to kill me, it would have been so easy.

Ari glanced at the kids, her eyes wide. "Crap," she whispered. "I could have hurt them."

There was something else she wasn't saying. I had a sudden fear, as I picked up on what it was, but I decided to leave it for the moment.

Rowan cleared her throat, glancing at me. She gave me a shake of the head. "But you didn't. They're fine. You know that in Moonshadow Bay, this sort of thing can happen anywhere. You grew up just fine. The children will be safe."

"Right," Ari said, but she didn't sound convinced. "Frieda, take over and lock up for the day. I need to take the kids home." Turning to me, she murmured, "I'll talk to you later," but she wouldn't meet my gaze and I knew, in my heart, that she blamed me for what had happened. Tears welled up in my eyes, but I merely nodded and motioned for Rowan to follow me. We went back to my house.

TARVISH WAS TALKING TO ESMARA WHEN WE ENTERED THE house. Surprised, I turned to my great-aunt. "He can see you?"

Of course he can. He's a Funtime demon. Apparently, when the dungeon master created him, she gave him the ability to see ghosts. Esmara looked delighted.

"Well, that helps matters," I said, dropping into a chair by the table. "I suppose the first thing to do is figure out if the shadow man is still in the house. Then figure out who gave me that mirror." I paused, then asked, "Do you think the Covenant of Chaos is responsible?"

Rowan shook her head. "No, I don't. Here's the thing. The shadow man has had you marked since you were a child. Back then, the Covenant of Chaos had no clue if you were going to be a problem. They probably didn't know you existed at that point. They go after bigger fish. While they targeted the Crystal Cauldron through Daya, they aren't going to take such a roundabout way for you, especially with the unpredictable nature of shadow people. I can guarantee you, shadow people won't put themselves out for any mortal, chaos magician or not."

"Then where did the mirror come from?" I pointed to where it sat on the table. "I'd like to junk it, but I have a feeling that's not going to deter the shadow man."

Tarvish walked over and picked up the mirror before I could tell him not to do that. He held it up, staring into it. "The mirror's magical, that's a given, but there's something... almost *carnivalish* about this. Is that even a word?"

I wasn't sure, but I understood what he meant. "That's how I felt when I was in the nexus house. It felt like I was in a fun house. You know those horror movies where it feels like you're running and your target keeps telescoping out?"

"We need to talk to Teran," Rowan said. "Call her."

I called Teran, who picked up on the first ring, and asked her to come over. She said to give her half an hour. I turned back to Rowan and Tarvish. Esmara was sitting at the table now, her elbow partially through the table.

"I'm going to lose Ari over this, aren't I?" While the shadow man was my main problem, I couldn't help it—I had to talk about my worries out. "She's afraid that being around me will endanger the kids." I hung my head, feeling like a failure. "She's my best friend. She stood by me when I was with Ellison and I turned my back on everything because he forced me to."

Rowan crossed her arms and worried her lower lip. After a

73

moment, she said, "If that happens, it won't be forever. But Ari's right to protect the children. They aren't witchblood, they're shifters. They don't have protection against magic. I had to give up your father to protect him. That was harder than anything else I ever did."

I felt like Rowan had smacked me, but I wasn't going to argue. When she made a stand, she made a stand, and nothing could shake her. Feeling both chastised and melancholy, I decided to change the subject until Ari and I had a chance to process what had happened.

"So what do we do first? I kind of want to run a sweep through the house but I'm leaving this up to your judgment. Where did the mirror come from? I suppose that's one of the biggest questions. And is the shadow man still in my house?" I had finally managed to stop calling it Killian's house—now that we were married and he had put me onto the deed.

"As soon as Teran gets here, we'll discuss the next step." Rowan glanced over at Tarvish, who had both cats on his lap. Esmara was still holding the circle, and she was quietly watching the Funtime demon as he cooed over Xi and Klaus. "He's such a sucker for cats."

"He seems pretty fond of you, too," I said.

"Yeah," Rowan said, keeping her voice low. "I have to admit, he's the only man I've ever considered long-term relationship material. Your grandfather... There was no way it would have worked out, even had Farlow been single."

"You think you might end up with a ring?" I asked. Tarvish was absorbed in playing with the cats and I doubted if he would have heard a thunderstorm had one developed directly over his head.

Rowan chuckled. "He's already asked. I told him I'm not ready for that kind of a commitment, but we can talk about it in another year, if things are still good between us. He was satisfied with my answer."

"Well then, I guess we wait and see—" I paused as a knock at the kitchen door announced Teran's arrival. I ushered her in and she sat with us at the table. I told her about the morning.

"A walk-in, according to Rebecca, possessed Ari. Rebecca blasted the demon out of existence. As far as I can tell, the shadow man fled, but I'd like to know if he's still in the house. We have to do something to that mirror to stop this from happening again."

Teran nodded. "We can't destroy the mirror until we use it to destroy the shadow man who has attached himself to you. You have to use it to enter the portal house."

"To clarify," Rowan said. "I'm sorry, January, but *you're* the one who will have to face him. Teran and I can block and banish him but as soon as the wards fade, he'll be able to return. There's only one way to permanently put him out of your misery, and that's for you to trace him into the nexus and destroy him, using the energy from the realm of light."

"I don't know how to do that," I said, terrified.

"We'll teach you," Teran said. "I hoped that he had forgotten about you, but I suppose they never fully forget when they sink their teeth into one of their marks."

"What happens when a person dies? One who's been marked?"

"For most people, the shadow man can then pursue them freely in the afterlife, which is why it's always best to end the connection while you're still alive. But you've been claimed by Druantia, so I have no idea how that would play out after your death. I'd rather not find out," Rowan said.

Tarvish suddenly broke into the conversation and I wondered how much he had heard of it. "As to how the mirror got here, I can venture a guess."

"Do tell," Teran said. "If we can figure it out, that may help our case."

Tarvish pointed toward the mirror. "That's not an ordinary mirror, obviously, but I think it's more than just a static portal. I think it's like a mimic in Dungeons and Dragons. But instead of being a sentient creature posing as an object, it's a sentient *portal* disguised as a mirror."

"Say what?" I turned to Tarvish, bewildered. "*Mimic?*"

"In the game, and in my memories since I was created to be part of a game, mimics are monsters that can assume the form of objects—like a table or a treasure chest. A lot of dungeon parties lost their lives by trying to open a random treasure chest—"

I could see Tarvish was settling in to tell us a bunch of stories from his time before he ended up in our world. While they were always entertaining, right now, we didn't have time for them.

"Okay, so what makes you think there are portal creatures?"

"Because there *are*," Rowan said. "I haven't heard a lot about them, but some portals are so ancient and so active that they develop a rudimentary form of intelligence. They can be harnessed and used by more intelligent beings. Which means there's a chance the shadow man created or captured his mirror."

"A dream… I had a dream a few months back, and I remember the mirror and the portal house from that dream. Maybe I tuned into him and saw what he was doing, or he tuned into me and got the idea, or something?" Something inside began sounding an alarm so loud that I knew I was on the right track.

"The migraines—they could have broadcast your energy far and wide," Teran said. "Since you've had to start casting spells and reading tarot over the past couple months, my guess is that the activity lit you up, and he remembered you—you caught his notice."

Rowan snapped her fingers. "She's right. I know she's right."

"Then what do I do? Can the mirror hear us? Can it talk to the shadow man?" I looked over at the mirror, which had somehow taken on a sinister look. The snakes seemed venomous now, and the thorns of the roses, sharp and barbed.

"I don't know about that," Rowan said. "I'll start working on a spell. Meanwhile, Teran and I will search through the house to see if we can find the shadow man. My guess is that he's not here right now. He's probably hiding, biding his time to when he can get to you. Tarvish, watch January, just in case."

As my grandmother and aunt prepared to search the house, I took another look at the mirror, although I avoided looking directly into it. Given the demon that had come through to possess Ari, who knew what else lurked behind the glass? I had no intention of finding out what might be waiting on the other side.

CHAPTER NINE

Tarvish and I sat at the table. I sighed. I hated feeling that others were rescuing me. "What's bothering you?" he asked. The cats had curled up on his lap and were sound asleep. He was definitely a first-rate cat whisperer.

"Rowan and Teran are checking out the house. I wasn't able to keep that thing from possessing Ari. I can't control my migraines. I feel like I've lost control of my life and I'm causing everybody so much trouble. Maybe I could have taken up practicing more magic after I left home, but instead, I let Ellison run things. I've never run my life, I've let it run me." I glanced at him. "I'm sorry, I..."

"I get it," he said. "I feel like that too. I can't go back to where I came from or I'll cease to exist. I was created as a figment of someone's imagination and every recollection I have from my days before you downloaded me off the net is an artificial memory. Without your help, I wouldn't exist— not in actual form. I don't have an option. I can never return to my origin because it's all so many squiggles on a piece of paper." He shrugged. "It was hard at first, but I've managed to accept my life as it is. But I have the choice of what to do now."

"I think I'm still fighting against the ERS. I thought I'd accepted the way my life changed, but I keep tripping over my own feet. And if I'm honest, I'm still angry. I'm angry at my mother. I'm angry at myself. And I feel like a song on repeat." I sighed. "I'm afraid my friends will get tired of listening to me, and I wouldn't blame them. But keeping all my feelings inside isn't serving me well, either."

Tarvish cautiously shifted in his chair. He was big—very big—and he was always aware that he might be one movement away from landing on the floor. He wasn't fat, but Funtime demons were built like tanks.

"You can call me to vent, whenever you need to. I won't get tired of listening, and I do understand." He leaned forward, cautious to avoid waking the cats. "Seriously—I'd like to help."

I knew Tarvish had a heart of gold, but the warmth in his voice washed over me and I realized why my grandmother liked being around him.

"Thanks. I'll take you up on that, I think—and you can call me too. I'll listen. Our situations are different, yes, but I can see how you might need an outside source to talk to. Maybe I need to talk to a therapist, too." I had thought about going to therapy for a while now, but each time I started to make the initial call, I'd backed away, thinking that I could handle it on my own.

"I'm going to add something else. Yes, you're sitting back while Teran and Rowan search the house, but your grandmother was right. Once she comes up with a spell, it will be *you* having to go in to take care of the shadow man. You'll be taking him on directly. If that's not looking out for yourself, what is?"

I stared at him. "You're right. And...I guess everybody needs help."

"They're helping you so that you can help yourself. Haven't you ever done that for someone?"

Esmara smiled. She was still there, though she had remained silent through our discussion. But now she said, *Tarvish is smart. You'd do well to pay attention to him. And you do know, you can always talk to me if nobody wants to listen.*

I ducked my head. "I know."

"Your great-aunt is a smart woman." Tarvish grinned.

"It's going to take me some time to remember that you can hear Esmara."

"I thought about whether I should tell you, then decided just to wait till the subject arose. And today, it did. I'd never want you to be embarrassed if you found out in a roundabout way."

A few minutes later, Rowan and Teran reappeared.

"He's not here, not at the moment," my grandmother said. "We need to prepare you to face him. Until then, I'm taking the mirror home with me. That way if he comes through, he'll be in my territory. I'll create a spell tonight. You should be safe if I have the mirror. Get a good night's sleep because tomorrow, I'll be back with the spell and components you need. It's time to put an end to this."

"Can Esmara help me somehow?" I asked.

"She can, but in the end, you need to be the one to face him. Once he's destroyed, the mark on you will disappear." Rowan stood, motioning to Tarvish. "All right, enough kitten sitting. Let's go." She shouldered her bag and, giving me a peck on the forehead, headed for the door, followed by Tarvish, who was carrying the mirror.

As they left, I thought about running next door to talk to Ari but decided to let her be for the moment. I wasn't sure I was ready to hear what she had to say.

After texting Tad that I'd be taking the entire day off after all, I rinsed the dishes and stacked them in the dishwasher. I was antsy, wanting to get the show on the road, but I couldn't until Rowan had created the spell for me, so I hauled out the vacuum cleaner and cleaned the rugs and floors. Then I scooped the litter boxes, cleaned the bathrooms, and shortly before lunch, I made a pot of spaghetti and watched one of my favorite shows on my iPad as I ate lunch.

The house was quiet, the cats were snoozing, and I was bored. I turned off the show and peeked out the window. It was snowing lightly and the afternoon had that silvery light that came with winter snowfall, and I decided to go out for a walk. I slid on my winter jacket and my non-slip boots, wrapped a muffler around my ears and neck, and then slid my hands into winter gloves. After making sure the stove was off and that the food was in the fridge, I headed out the back door.

The snow fluttered down, delicate flakes barely kissing the ground. There was enough snow already built up, and it was cold enough that they stuck. It was set to snow for quite a while, and I held out my hands, catching the flakes on my gloves. I walked through the empty raised beds, covered with leaves and then a layer of snow. What would I grow this year? Would I have the time and energy to garden?

I brushed the fresh snow off of the bench at the trailhead that led into the Mystic Wood, and sat down, huddling against the chill.

"Are you all right?"

Startled, I glanced over at a nearby huckleberry bush. Rebecca peeked out from behind the branches, again in her little-girl guise. She slipped out into the open and stood there, watching me.

"Hey, Rebecca. Thank you again for your help. I'll ask Killian to grill you up a couple racks of ribs this weekend, if that's soon enough." I pulled my hood up to cover my head and ears.

"That's fine. I like them a lot." Rebecca paused, then said, "What are you going to do?"

I wondered how much she knew. "I'm going to find the shadow man and destroy him. My grandmother will be helping me."

"Your grandmother is quite capable of teaching you to go up against the shadow people."

"What was that thing that possessed Ari?" I asked.

Rebecca shrugged, leaning against a fence post. She looked like she should be freezing, but she didn't seem to notice the cold.

"A walk-in. They can possess people who aren't prepared against them. They have no physical form other than when they've 'walked in' to others' bodies. They're lower-level demons. I'm an imp, a minor demon, but there are plenty of demons far lower than me. Walk-ins belong to a seething pool of entities that are constantly hungry. You can barely consider them individuals, until they've broken off from the main stem. Then they can start growing on an individual level as long as they feed."

"Obviously, I have a lot to learn about demons." I hesitated, wondering how far I could trust Rebecca.

"You're better off not knowing," she said. "Now, I have things to do. Go back inside. It's too cold out here for the likes of you." She turned, sauntering down the trail.

Killian texted me that he'd be home early. I decided to wait until then to tell him about the demon. Meanwhile, I screwed up my courage and headed over to Ari's salon with a basket of muffins. As I opened the door, she was sweeping up some hair.

"Hey, I thought you could use a pick-me-up." I held out the muffins.

Ari leaned on her broom. "Thanks. I could. Donna took the kids home for the afternoon and I'm just waiting for my last client." She motioned me in. "She's not due for half an hour. Come in. We need to talk."

Apprehensive, I joined her at the kitchen table. She poured us coffee as I arranged the muffins on a plate. "I made them—they're cinnamon crumble."

"They smell good," she said, handing me a mug as she set the cream and sugar on the table. "So...this morning..."

"Yeah, I suppose we should talk about it," I said. "I don't want to, but we have to at some point."

"I'm sorry if I hurt your feelings, but this morning it finally hit me. I'm now mother to two children who've already had their world ripped out from under them once. I'm not going to tell Meagan what happened today, because if I did, she'd put her foot down and insist that I keep the kids away from you, even though she thinks the world of you." Ari stared into her coffee. "I won't tell her, but I have to be careful. You live in a dangerous world, January—"

"We *all* do. Moonshadow Bay's not the safest town around. The Mystic Wood guarantees that. Hell, no place in this world is safe. Not Seattle. Not Bellingham. Not Moonshadow Bay. And I didn't invite the walk-in to possess you—"

"No, but if I hadn't walked into your house, it wouldn't have had a chance to jump me. And look at Mothman—"

"That's not fair! I had nothing to do with inviting

Mothman into the area. Mothman controls his own comings and goings and he could have targeted you regardless of whether I was around. He targeted others and I had no connection to them."

She sighed. "All right, I'll give you that one. But I *can't* put myself in any extra danger. I walk over to your house and boom, a demon possesses me. You work in a dangerous job and…" She looked away. "You're not going to like this, but I have to think of my family. I'm going to look for a new place for my salon. For now, I'll go back to using my house, but I'll find a new space. Don't worry—I'll pay you for the rest of the lease. And I'll renovate the house back to a house instead of a salon, but I feel that…"

I flushed, feeling embarrassed and angry and hurt. I understood her reasons, but that didn't make them any easier. I knew I needed to get out of there before I blew up. "Forget the lease. If this is what you want, just restore the house back to being a house." I set my coffee mug on the table and stood. "But restore it as soon as you can, so I can find another renter."

"Please don't be upset—" she started.

I threw on my coat. "Listen, I understand your fears. I do," I said, meeting her gaze. "But don't you *dare* ask me to act like this doesn't hurt. You have to do what you have to do. And I *know* that I pulled away when I married Ellison, with far less reason. That was a crummy thing for me to do. But if this is about evening the score—"

"Not at all! January, we can still be best friends. We'll just meet away from your house."

"Because my house is filled with ghosts, right? Because my husband's a big scary shifter, nothing like your wife—who's an even *bigger* predator."

"This has nothing to do with Meagan and Killian. No, it's *not* your fault the shadow man marked you—but the fallout is dangerous. And it goes beyond us. I'm leaving the Crystal Cauldron. The Covenant of Chaos is dangerous, and I won't let them near my kids." She bristled, and I could hear the defensiveness in her voice.

I met her gaze, not bothering to wipe away the tears. "Go. Take care of your babies. They need you. But if you expect me to be all rah-rah, then think again. I don't have enough spoons to pretend." A twinge in my forehead alerted me. "It feels like my migraine's returning. I'm heading home before it hits. Email me when you decide to vacate the house." I stood, biting my lip so hard that it was bleeding—I could taste the blood on my tongue.

"January—" Ari burst into tears. "Do you want me to help you home? How fast is the headache coming on?"

I almost said yes, but then shook my head. "I'll be fine." Softening my voice, I added, "Whether or not you believe me, I *do* understand. And I *do* know you're between a rock and a hard place. Those babies need you more than I do, more than anybody else does. Give them my love. I don't suppose I'll get to see them anymore..."

Before she could say anything, I turned and almost ran out the door. By the time I ran across the driveway, slipping twice, and slammed the door behind me, I was crying full force. I stripped off my coat and gloves, tossing them onto the sofa, then headed straight into the bedroom, stopping to grab my medication on the way.

MIGRAINE IS REBOUNDING AND I'M HEADED TO BED. I CAN'T EVEN BEGIN TO TEXT ABOUT IT. PLEASE DON'T BE LATE TONIGHT. I NEED YOU. After texting Killian, I tossed the phone on the bed and stripped, pulling my nightie over my head. I wouldn't be doing any spell work tonight, that was for sure. I shoved my feet under the covers and leaned back against the headboard. Xi jumped up on my lap, nuzzling me.

Are you okay? She rubbed her cheek against mine, purring.

"I'm sad, little one. And I don't feel good." I broke into tears, pulling her to me. She relaxed into my hug, letting me bury my face in her coat.

I love you, was all the tortie said. And that was all I needed.

"January! Are you awake?" Killian's voice echoed from the foyer.

I hadn't fallen asleep. In fact, I was watching an old black and white movie on TV, with the sound turned low and the lights dimmed. It was still enough to hurt my head, but I didn't want to be alone with my thoughts. I turned off the TV as Killian hurried into the bedroom, a worried look on his face.

"Sweetheart, are you all right?" He settled on the bed next to me, taking my hand. "How bad is the headache?"

"It's not great, but I've managed to keep it at bay." I leaned against his shoulder. "Today was bad. Very bad."

"I know," he whispered, wrapping his arm around me. "Ari texted me."

For some reason, that made me irrationally angry. "She couldn't let me tell you myself?"

"She was worried—she told me about your headache returning."

"That's not her place. What else did she tell you?" I asked.

"Not much, just that you two had an argument." He kissed me. "What was it about?"

"It's not an argument. It's... I'm losing her, and I have to let her go. She's feeling guilty and trying to gaslight my feelings." I paused, then said, "Maybe not gaslight, but she doesn't want to hear why I'm upset because that makes her feel more guilty. It's a no-win situation."

As he took off his shoes and crawled under the covers with me, I told him everything that had happened, from the demon possessing Ari to Rebecca saving our asses to the conversation that had shattered our friendship.

"So, you owe Rebecca a couple sides of ribs—and make them juicy and thick with sauce. She came through for us in a way I never expected. And we'll have to look for somebody to rent the house once Ari turns it back into an actual house." I shrugged.

"Well, I certainly see why your migraine is coming back. I'm sorry about Ari. There's nothing I can say. You're right— it's a no-win situation." He pulled me into the nook of his arm.

"Then you think I'm losing her, too? I'm not being melo-dramatic?"

"No, sweetheart. You're not. And no one can take her place, but I love you, and I'm always going to be here for you."

I looked up at him, infinitely grateful that he was my husband, that we had found each other. I might be losing Ari, but at least I had Killian, and wolf shifters mated for life. Divorce was seldom an option, except for in cases of abuse or alienation of affections.

"Thank you," I said, kissing him back. "I'm going to need you more over the next few months, until I adjust."

At that moment, my phone rang. It was Rowan. "Hello?"

"Hey, I have a spell ready for you. I'll bring it over tomorrow morning. It's too late tonight." Rowan's voice was firm, but I could hear the worry behind her words.

"I'll see you at nine-thirty, then. I'm fighting another migraine tonight. I'll tell you all about it tomorrow morning."

As Rowan hung up, I stared at my phone. Tomorrow I'd attempt to cut the cords connecting me to the shadow man. It occurred to me that over the past few years I'd learned to let so many things go. And now, it was time to do that again. But I wasn't sure if I was talking about my connection to the shadow man, or my friendship with Ari.

CHAPTER TEN

Morning came, and I felt a little better. Killian and I'd talked late into the night. Not about Ari or the demon or anything to do with that, but about our future and what we wanted in the years to come.

"So, shall we go check out the cabin next weekend? The one Nonny left to you?"

I had nodded, wiping my tears. "Let's take Teran. I'll ask Tarvish to check in on the cats."

"That sounds like fun. Honestly, I love the idea of a vacation cabin." He paused, then said, "How big is it?"

"Three bedrooms, with a big living room."

"How about asking Tad, Caitlin, and Hank along, too? We can make everybody fit."

I knew what he was doing, and I appreciated it more than I could express. "I think they'd like that—especially Hank."

"Good. Oh, another thing. Tally asked if we could watch

the girls next month. She and Les would like to get away for a weekend near Valentine's Day," he said.

"She trusts me with them?" I asked, feeling bitter, but then I reined it in. Tally was wonderful and I was grateful that she treated me like a sister. "Of course we'll help. We're their aunt and uncle. But I'm not very conversant with babies, so..."

"We can manage for one weekend. I'll diaper them, if you don't mind heating up the formula." He entwined his fingers in mine. "Thank you. It would mean a lot to them."

Tally was Killian's sister, and she had given birth to twin girls about six months ago. Victoria and Leanna were adorable, for babies, and we often got together with Tally and Les for dinner. They had moved to Moonshadow Bay for Les's new job, and it also meant that Killian and Tally could spend more time together.

"Do they know where they're going?" I asked.

Killian shook his head. "No, they haven't decided yet. It can't be anyplace expensive, though. They're on a tight budget."

I smiled. "Why don't we give them a weekend at a spa? There's a nice one in Bellingham. They have couples' massages, aqua therapy, a sauna, and a three-star restaurant. Ask Tally if they'd like that and we'll book them a room for their choice of weekend."

"There are so many reasons why I love you. That you love my family is one more wonderful perk. That would be wonderful. I'll call Tally in the morning and work things out. And for what it's worth, Tally told me that she considers you the sister she's always wanted."

On that note, we snuggled down for a few hours of sleep, and my dreams were filled with family and Killian, and no sign of the shadow man.

COME MORNING, THE MIGRAINE HAD BACKED AWAY. I glanced over at my house and caught my breath. Ari already had the contractor there. Part of me had hoped it was a bad dream, but I had to face the facts that it wasn't. Life was changing, and the only control I had was how I reacted. Steeling myself, I told Killian I'd be back and headed next door.

Ari looked startled as I appeared in the doorway, but I just nodded to the contractor.

"Hi, I'm the owner. Once you have an estimate for how long it will take to renovate the house, let me know so I can approve the plans, and so I can schedule out a timeframe for renting it out." I couldn't look at Ari or I'd start crying again, so I focused on the wall as I said, "I'll charge you rent until the work is finished, but as I said yesterday, I won't hold you to the lease." I kept my tone even and as friendly as I could.

"That's good of you," Ari said, sounding stung. "I'll have the work done as quickly as we can."

The contractor seemed to realize he was in the middle of a war and he had to do his best to play Switzerland.

I turned my attention to him. "If you'll consult with me before you paint, I'll give you a list of colors. I suppose that's everything," I said, turning toward the door.

"January, please—can I talk to you for a moment?" Ari said.

I didn't turn around. "I'm sorry, I have things to do. Email me." And I walked out of the house, trying to let go of the past.

AT PROMPTLY NINE-THIRTY, ROWAN AND TERAN APPEARED. Tarvish accompanied them. I held my breath as they set out equipment on the dining room table. Esmara appeared. Tarvish and I waved to her.

"Esmara, can you cast a circle in the guest room and we'll put Xi and Klaus in there to keep them safe?" I asked.

Of course. But I think you may want Teran to do that instead.

"Why?" I glanced over at Rowan. "Esmara said it might be better to have Teran guard the cats."

"Yes, she's right. Esmara apparently visited me last night when I called on her. Tarvish said she was watching and approved of what I was thinking. She's going to help you in the nexus—she can easily enter it with you. So she can't hold the circle outside."

I turned to Esmara. "You're going to be there with me? That makes me feel better!" I turned to Teran. "Then would you set up a circle in the guest room?"

"I'm on it," she said. "Tarvish, can you corral the cats for me and bring them in?"

While they headed off for the second floor, I watched Rowan. She had brought the mirror with her, wrapped in red cloth, tied with a black cord. She had also brought a large crystal ball—it was as big as a bowling ball and as heavy as one—and settled it onto a large stand. Beside it, she placed her dagger, a wand, a sage stick, a large bell, and a small gold box that radiated with energy.

"What's in that?" I pointed to the box.

"A small nodule of pure light essence, trapped in a ring. Go get your sunglasses."

I opened a drawer in the foyer table where Killian and I kept our sunglasses when we weren't using them—which was most of the year—and pulled out my Ray-Bans. As I carried them back to the kitchen, Rowan had finished setting up. She had put the mirror in the center of a ring of salt and grave-yard dust in the middle of the table.

"How do we do this?" I asked.

"I'll cast a circle around this room, one strong enough to keep the shadow man from escaping into the rest of the house. I've already cast a circle around the mirror, which will double the protection. He shouldn't be able to get out of the portal house, but if he does, then the second circle will put a stop to him getting away from us."

"What should I get of my equipment?"

"Your athame. And I'm going to give you something that belonged to my mother. She was an earth-based witch, too, so her ritual necklace never worked for me. She was a priestess, dedicated to Cerridwen. I never went the route of pledging myself to a god or goddess, but she was devout. You're more like her than I realized." She handed me a black velvet box.

I opened it, staring at the sterling silver pentacle. Two inches in diameter, the pentacle had an emerald cabochon in the center. It was clear green, as green as my eyes, and the pentacle was on a silver chain.

"This is beautiful. Are you sure you want me to wear it?" I asked.

"No, I want you to *have* it. I've cleansed it of Cerridwen's energy, so you can dedicate it to Druantia. I think…she has plans for you and this is only the beginning." Rowan caught my gaze. "Things happen for a reason, most of the time. There's a reason you're facing the shadow man, and that you found yourself in the portal house. There's a reason Ari's pulling back. You just have to give the future grace so that it can happen as it needs to."

As she spoke, an odd peace settled in my heart and I felt my anger and hurt lift and float away. I draped the pentacle around my neck, and a cool energy—like the forest cloaked in mist and dew—swept over me. At that moment, I felt gentle hands on my shoulders, and then as quickly as the presence was there, it was gone again.

"Rowan, I felt hands—"

"My mother. She stays near me and I can feel her here now. I don't talk about my family often because when I left Ireland, I thought I would be going home again to visit, but my mother and father died in a housefire before I could."

I hadn't ever asked about Rowan's family, I'd been so caught up in the drama that surrounded my maternal side. Now, though, it dawned on me that my heritage really did involve far more than the Ladies, far more than Colleen and her secrets. And the two were entwined.

"Why did you come to the US?"

"I came with Colleen and Brian. We, along with a few others, were instructed by the Court Magika to establish Moonshadow Bay. So we followed instructions. Colleen and Brian had joined the coven over in Ireland, along with me. I was chosen to lead the Crystal Cauldron here." She hesitated, then added, "I didn't know Colleen and Brian well while we lived in Ireland, but Brian and I struck up a friendship on the boat ride over. Once we settled the town, I discovered I liked Colleen a lot more."

"What was your mother's name?" I played with the necklace. It tingled in my fingers, making me smile. "And your father?"

"My mother's name was Willow. My father's name was Falcon." She paused, then added, "There are secrets to my family that you will learn as you go along. But it explains a lot about why your magic is so strong. Your connections to the dead come through your maternal line, but your connections to the earth, and the reason the Fae helped you with Bigfoot, come from my line."

I stared at her. There were definitely things she wasn't

telling me about her family, but I knew Rowan well enough to understand that I'd find out when she thought I was ready.

"I'll get my dagger," I said. As I retrieved it from my ritual room, I could feel Druantia near me. She seemed to fixate on the necklace, and I paused, listening to her prompting. I took off the necklace and held it out to the altar. Usually, I preferred to create more ceremony, but sometimes, a witch had to work by the seat of her broomstick.

"I dedicate this necklace to you, Lady Druantia, to represent and hold the bond between us. When I wear this, I wear it in honor of you, and in honor of our connection." Even as I spoke, I could feel her pouring her energy into the pentacle, and when I draped it around my neck again, she was there, with me, standing at my back.

I picked up my dagger. It had a bronze blade, and the bog oak hilt was inlaid with malachite, moss agate, peridot, and citrine cabochons, and had a Celtic triskelion engraved on it. The bog oak was from Ireland, over three thousand years old and dark black.

As I reentered the kitchen, Rowan looked up, her eyes widening. "She liked the necklace?"

"You felt that? Druantia claimed it right away. I can feel her with me."

"That's a good thing. She'll be with you in this." Rowan looked around. "I guess we're ready. Do you need anything first? Food to ground you?"

"I ate breakfast. I'll run to the restroom and then we can begin. But you have to tell me how to use that ring."

"I'll lay out everything while you're gone."

As I headed to the bathroom, I realized this was it—I was facing down a nightmare from childhood, hopefully to put an end to it.

ROWAN HANDED ME THE SUNGLASSES WHEN I RETURNED. She was wearing a pair herself, and so was Tarvish. "Put these on. You need to before I open the box with the ring in it. Don't take them off, even inside the nexus. You could be blinded otherwise."

I put them on and then she opened the box. The ring was so bright, even with my sunglasses, that it was difficult to look at. It radiated white-hot light, neon bright like the sun. As she held it out, motioning me to hold up my finger, I hesitated.

"Will it burn?"

"No, not in the small concentration that was forged into the metal. One small drop of essence in there created this powerful of a ring."

I held out my hand and she slid the ring on my finger. It hit me like a sledgehammer, almost knocking me back, the energy was so intense. The ring felt incredibly heavy, for coming from a realm labeled the "light realm."

"How do I use it?"

"When you encounter the shadow man, you have to stab him with your athame, using the hand wearing the ring. So make certain it's your dominant hand."

"I'm left-handed, but I use knives and scissors with my right," I said. The ring was on my right ring finger. "I should be good. What happens if I get too close to him?"

"He can latch on and try to drain you. So you'll have to work fast."

"How will I call him out?" I asked.

"I think...when you get inside the nexus, challenge him. He'll hear you, and he'll probably be eager to face you. But the minute you see him, you have to go after him because if he senses the light ring, he may try to flee."

That's where I come in, Esmara said. She appeared by my shoulder. *I'll go in with you and hide, then when he comes to you, I'll try to block his avenues of escape. I'm strong enough that he'll be wary about confronting me.*

"Then I guess we're ready." I closed my eyes, both nervous and eager. "Text Killian and tell him what we're doing. I want him to be prepared."

"Take hold of your dagger and get ready. When I open the mirror, look into it and see the room where you were before. I can feel that the mirror's angry, and it should suck you right in once I remove the bindings."

Rowan carried the mirror over to where I was sitting. I took a deep breath as she began to open the bindings. Esmara stood behind me.

"Ready?" Rowan asked.

I nodded. "I'm ready."

She unwrapped the mirror. As I looked deep into my own reflection, visualizing the nexus, the energy around me began to grow. Another moment, and everything disappeared as I felt myself being yanked into the glass. The mirror was awake, all right, and I was on my way.

Within seconds, I found myself in the portal house again, only this time I knew what was going on, and Esmara was there with me. I started to take off my sunglasses, the illumination was so dark, but Esmara shook her head and I stopped.

"That's right, I forgot. All right, let me summon him. I want this over with," I said. This time, as with the first time I was ever in this space, I saw the mirror on the wall. I walked up to it and gazed at my reflection. "If you want me, come get me," I said, hiding my hands behind my back. "I'm waiting, coward."

Apparently, the shadow man didn't like being called a coward, because the next moment, I felt something barreling toward us. Esmara peeked around the corner of the nook and then motioned for me to get ready.

And then, he was there, in front of me. I jumped. I'd been ready, but you're never, ever fully ready when gearing up for battle. Before I could move, he grabbed me by the throat and leaned near. I could feel tendrils of darkness begin to penetrate my skin, corkscrewing into my flesh.

Gasping, I swatted at him, trying to push him back, but he was draining me, sucking away my energy and life force. I struggled to keep my focus, even as it felt like he was eating away at my essence. I struggled to keep conscious, but I could feel myself slipping. I couldn't raise my hands, couldn't touch him even though I was within easy reach. Instead, it was as though massive hoses had reamed their way into me from all angles and were now siphoning off every ounce of life that flowed through my body.

Esmara screeched, loud as a banshee, and the shadow man recoiled, letting go of me as he covered where his ears should be. I yanked away, whirling out of his grasp. As I danced away, the tendrils ripped out of me like roots out of the earth. The shadow man let out a low hiss, focusing on me again. Esmara rushed at him, her eyes aflame. I'd never seen her look so fierce, and for the first time, she wore the skull of death on her face, her features melting away, her locks flowing into flame. She charged him and he backed away cautiously.

I took the opportunity to bring out my dagger. My hand glowed and I realized it was the ring, shimmering as bright as the sun.

The shadow man cried out, turning as soon as he caught sight of my hand, but Esmara was on the other side of him, blocking his way.

He swung at her and she gasped as he punched her deep in the gut. For a moment, her presence wavered, but before he could run, she formed again, stronger than before. She looked like a creature of the grave, not my great-aunt. A creature of nightmares, she dropped her head back, letting out another ear-piercing scream. It hit me in the solar plexus, but it seemed to rip *through* the shadow man, and he blinked in and out.

I charged forward, raising my dagger. As I brought it down, I whispered an incantation that suddenly came to me.

Mother of Earth, Mother of Birth,
Mistress of Stones, Crystals, and Bones,
Mother of Creation, Mistress of Destruction,
Here my plea, Feed your energy through me.

And Druantia was there, behind the dagger, behind my shoulder, feeding me strength as I plunged the dagger into him. The light from the ring infused the blade, and now it spread through the shadow man, like cracks in a window, shattering his darkness with a web that spread all through his body.

Like I'd seen when Rebecca destroyed the walk-in, so the shadow man froze as the energy permeated him, and then— without a whisper—he dissolved into dust that fell to the floor.

I dropped my arm. Esmara leaned over me.

Are you all right? she asked, back to her usual form.

But I'd seen her *true* nature, beneath the gracious aunt that I knew so well. She was more powerful than I ever imagined. I was beginning to realize that all my preconceptions were surface level and that I was surrounded by creatures and beings who lived beyond the borders of the physical world around me. And that included my own self. I was more than my body, I was more than my daily routine—so *much* more. Everything lived on multiple levels, and it was up to us to dig for the truth of how deep they went.

Esmara helped me stand, and I turned to her. "I need to destroy the mirror," I said.

She nodded. "Yes, you do. Strike it with the dagger, using the energy from the ring."

And so I did. I turned to the mirror and brought my dagger up, hitting it square in the center. As a thousand shards of glass began to rain down around us, I closed my eyes, raising my face to the stars, which now appeared above us. As the heavens opened around us, I felt myself begin to spin, until I was soaring into the sky. Then before I could go too far out, I heard someone calling my name, and I turned, coasting toward the direction I had come.

Within seconds, I slammed back into my body, so hard it hurt. I opened my eyes. The mirror was shattered, on the table. Esmara was standing there. My dagger was covered with an oily black substance. And the ring of light was shining with the light of a thousand suns.

CHAPTER ELEVEN

WE WERE SITTING IN FRONT OF THE FIREPLACE, STARING AT the fire. I had returned from offering Rebecca three sides of ribs—an extra slab for the effort she had expended for me—and now, Killian and I snuggled by the crackling flames.

I felt better than I had in ages. While I still had energy reflux syndrome, it had lightened considerably since I had dislodged the shadow man's mark from my forehead. Now, Druantia's mark reigned, and I could feel her with every core of my being. She was in my heart and soul. It was like an awakening.

It was Saturday morning, and since the battle on Thursday, I'd felt an inordinate sense of peace, with everything and everybody.

"What are you thinking?" Killian asked.

"I'm thinking about Rowan, and what she told me about her family. And of Teran, and Ari, and all the magic that runs through my life. I don't know where I'm going from here, but it feels like doors have opened, and I think I'm ready to walk through them." I cupped a mug of mocha in my hands, sipping the sweet chocolate coffee.

"What about you and Ari?" he asked, stretching out on the sofa. I was sitting on the floor in front of him.

"Whatever is, will be. We'll come back together in time—Rowan reassured me of that. I wrote Ari an email yesterday, wishing her the best, and telling her that when she's ready, to contact me and we'll find our new path. I think it's best if we go our own ways for the immediate future. There's so much to learn, and Druantia wants my attention. Teran's going to help me, along with Rowan." I paused. "I'm taking a break from work. A short sabbatical until I figure out what I need to do. Tad understands. I have enough money so we won't be hurting."

"We won't be hurting anyway. I bought this house with cash. There's no mortgage. You'll have rental income. Do what you need to do. The only thing I ask is that you keep *me* in your future," he said, setting down his tablet. He patted the seat next to him. Xi and Klaus were stretched out on the back.

"I feel free in a way I never have. I didn't realize that the shadow man had such a hold on me," I said, leaning against him.

"Sometimes the damnedest things can keep us prisoner. But I'm glad you're free from him. What did you do with that ring?" he asked.

"Oh, I gave it back to Rowan. It's more aligned with her fire energy than my earth energy, or even the death magic that I use." I paused, then said, "Let's change the subject. What are you wearing tonight?"

"What do you mean?"

"I mean, it's not every day that you get inducted into the Pack as a second lieutenant. And I'll be there, cheering you on."

Killian smiled, kissing me softly. "I'll wear what all the other nominees do. Black suit pants, sports jacket, and loafers. Seriously, thank you for going."

"I'm as much a part of the Pack now as you are, since I'm your wife. I *want* to go. I want to watch you move ahead in your world...just as you've stood beside me as I've made changes." I stood, stretching. "Okay. I bought my dress this morning, and I guarantee you'll love it. Let's eat some lunch. And then we can take a long shower together, and spend the afternoon making love before we dress for the event."

Killian laughed and playfully smacked my ass. "Sex in the shower?" he asked. "Get your lovely ass into the bedroom."

As we headed toward the bedroom, I caught sight of the contractors next door. My house was going to be *my* house again, for better or worse. Ari had called me, and we'd had a cautious conversation focused on the renovations. I thought it was the first step to creating a bandage over the gaping wound in our friendship. But in time, the wound would heal.

Shaking off the melancholy mood, I went into the bedroom, stripping as I did so. Together with Killian, we'd forge a life together that was our own distinct path. I had the feeling it would look different than the one I'd imagined, but life was a constant series of steps and moves. If it wasn't, then we'd be walking among the dead. And neither one of us was ready for the grave.

FOR MORE OF THE MOONSHADOW BAY SERIES:
January Jaxson returns to the quirky town of Moonshadow Bay after her husband dumps her and steals their business, and within days she's working for Conjure Ink, a paranormal investigations agency, and exploring the potential of her hot new neighbor. Eleven books are currently available. You can preorder the second to the last Moonshadow Bay book—

Woodland Web—now! If you haven't read the other books in this series, begin with **Starlight Web**.

For more of the Starlight Hollow Series, you can preorder Elphyra's next books. Together with her red dragonette—Fancypants—she both protects *and* heats up the town in every sense of the word. Preorder the third book, **Starlight Demons**, now!

And if you love romantasy, you can preorder the first book in my **Winter's Spell Trilogy—Weaving Winter**—now. Dive into Asajia's world, where danger lurks around every corner, and where sometimes, it's safer to trust the Wolf than to trust the Prince.

For all the rest of my current and finished series, check out my State of the Series page, and you can also check the Bibliography at the end of this book, or check out my website at **Galenorn.com** and be sure and sign up for my **newsletter** to receive news about all my new releases. Also, you're welcome to join my YouTube Channel community.

QUALITY CONTROL: This work has been professionally edited and proofread. If you encounter any typos or formatting issues ONLY, please contact me through my **website** so they may be corrected. Otherwise, know that this book is in my style and voice and editorial suggestions will not be entertained. Thank you.

PLAYLIST

I often write to music, and DREAMER'S WEB was no
exception, but I took an entirely different approach. I
listened to a couple playlists on YouTube of music to focus by.
The two channels I used were:

- **Meditative Mind** (you can buy their music on
  Amazon): Their Hang Drum and Tabla music.
- **Chill Music Lab**.

BIOGRAPHY

New York Times, *Publishers Weekly*, and *USA Today* bestselling author Yasmine Galenorn writes urban fantasy and paranormal romance, and is the author of over one hundred books, including the Wild Hunt Series, the Fury Unbound Series, the Bewitching Bedlam Series, the Indigo Court Series, and the Otherworld Series, among others. She's also written nonfiction metaphysical books. She is the 2011 Career Achievement Award Winner in Urban Fantasy, given by RT Magazine. Yasmine has been in the Craft since 1980, is a shamanic witch and High Priestess. She describes her life as a blend of teacups and tattoos. She lives in Kirkland, WA, with her husband Samwise and their cats. Yasmine can be reached via her website at **Galenorn.com**. You can find all her links at her **LinkTree**.

Indie Releases Currently Available:

Moonshadow Bay Series:
   Starlight Web
   Midnight Web

Conjure Web
Harvest Web
Shadow Web
Weaver's Web
Crystal Web
Witch's Web
Cursed Web
Solstice Web
Dreamer's Web
Woodland Web

Winter's Spell Trilogy:
    Weaving Winter

Night Queen Series:
    Tattered Thorns
    Shattered Spells
    Fractured Flowers

Starlight Hollow Series:
    Starlight Hollow
    Starlight Dreams
    Starlight Demons

Magic Happens Series:
    Shadow Magic
    Charmed to Death

Hedge Dragon Series:
    The Poisoned Forest
    The Tangled Sky

The Wild Hunt Series:
    The Silver Stag

Oak & Thorns
Iron Bones
A Shadow of Crows
The Hallowed Hunt
The Silver Mist
Witching Hour
Witching Bones
A Sacred Magic
The Eternal Return
Sun Broken
Witching Moon
Autumn's Bane
Witching Time
Hunter's Moon
Witching Fire
Veil of Stars
Antlered Crown

Lily Bound Series
    Soul jacker

Chintz 'n China Series:
    Ghost of a Chance
    Legend of the Jade Dragon
    Murder Under a Mystic Moon
    A Harvest of Bones
    One Hex of a Wedding
    Holiday Spirits
    Well of Secrets
    Chintz 'n China Books, 1 – 3: Ghost of a Chance, Legend of the Jade Dragon, Murder Under A Mystic Moon
    Chintz 'n China Books, 4-6: A Harvest of Bones, One Hex of a Wedding, Holiday Spirits

Whisper Hollow Series:
    Autumn Thorns
    Shadow Silence
    The Phantom Queen

Bewitching Bedlam Series:
    Bewitching Bedlam
    Maudlin's Mayhem
    Siren's Song
    Witches Wild
    Casting Curses
    Demon's Delight
    Bedlam Calling: A Bewitching Bedlam Anthology
    Wish Factor (a prequel short story)
    Blood Music (a prequel novella)
    Blood Vengeance (a Bewitching Bedlam novella)
    Tiger Tails (a Bewitching Bedlam novella)

Fury Unbound Series:
    Fury Rising
    Fury's Magic
    Fury Awakened
    Fury Calling
    Fury's Mantle

Indigo Court Series:
    Night Myst
    Night Veil
    Night Seeker
    Night Vision
    Night's End
    Night Shivers
    Indigo Court Books, 1-3: Night Myst, Night Veil, Night Seeker (Boxed Set)

Indigo Court Books, 4-6: Night Vision, Night's End, Night Shivers (Boxed Set)

Otherworld Series:
    Moon Shimmers
    Harvest Song
    Blood Bonds
    Otherworld Tales: Volume 1
    Otherworld Tales: Volume 2
    For the rest of the Otherworld Series, see website at
Galenorn.com.

Bath and Body Series (originally under the name India Ink):
    Scent to Her Grave
    A Blush With Death
    Glossed and Found

Misc. Short Stories/Anthologies:
    The Longest Night (A Pagan Romance Novella)

Magickal Nonfiction: A Witch's Guide Series.
    Embracing the Moon
    Tarot Journeys
    Totem Magick

Manufactured by Amazon.ca
Bolton, ON

39245056R00066